WILEY'S REFRAIN

WILEY'S REFRAIN

LONO WAIWAIOLE

ST. MARTIN'S MINOTAUR

NEW YORK

www.minotaurbooks.com

Library of Congress Cataloging-in-Publication Data

Waiwaiole, Lono.
    Wiley's refrain / Lono Waiwaiole.—1st St. Martin's Minotaur ed.
        p. cm.
    ISBN 0-312-34909-2
    EAN 978-0-312-34909-7
    1. Wiley (Fictitious character : Waiwaiole)—Fiction. 2. Musicians—
Crimes against—Fiction. 3. Portland (Or.)—Fiction. 4. Poker players—
Fiction. 5. Hawaii—Fiction. I. Title.

PS3623.A425W55 2005
813'.6—dc22
                                                        2005047017

10   9   8   7   6   5   4   3   2

FOR BENJAMIN POKI'I WAIWAI'OLE
*The music man who gave me my first taste
of the blues—Aloha wau ia 'oe e Papa.*

ACKNOWLEDGMENTS

I am surrounded by people who know a good book when they see one and are happy to share their insight with me. They are Ben Sevier from St. Martin's Minotaur, who bought this book and promptly showed me how to make it better; Gina Maccoby, who loved it and promptly sold it; and early readers Kaila and Poeko in Hilo and Kulia and Gabe in Portland, who know Wiley well and like him anyway.

WILEY'S REFRAIN

ONE

I'm not sure if it started with the book in her hand or the scar on her face, but the origin didn't ultimately matter because the fact that it started at all turned out to be the significant thing.

And it might not have been either of those cues. Maybe it started because I arrived on the Big Island four hours early and a lifetime too late, only one of which I could do something about. Maybe it was just my talent for waiting; maybe my ability to kill four decades of my life before my first visit to my ancestral homeland led me to kill the four extra hours on my hands at exactly the right place.

Or maybe it was much more mundane than all of the above; maybe it was only what attracts men to women all the time—the way her hip was cocked while she studied the book in her hands, perhaps, or the way she tossed her long black hair over her shoulder when I got my first glimpse of the scar.

I hadn't been looking for a woman when I arrived in Hilo, of course. I had come expressly to rain on Danny Alexander's parade, and I didn't expect to have much trouble doing it even though the locals were grousing that the island was in the middle of a drought. I could have told them not to worry—I intended to generate enough precipitation to fill every catchment tank on the island.

If I had been inclined to tell anyone anything, that is, which I was not. My inclination was to keep my mouth shut and my ears open, and that's what I did as I walked from the plane to my rental car—a journey that requires fewer steps at Hilo International than anywhere else I have ever been. A round brown woman with a deep smile checked me in when I got to her counter, and she handed me my paperwork and a set of keys no more than twenty minutes after my plane had rolled to a stop at the terminal.

"Welcome home," she said, apparently believing the face in front of her more than the Oregon driver's license. I could understand her confusion—I looked a lot like many of the people milling around in the pickup area behind me. But I was a *long* way from home, just like Dannyboy, and I was going to be even farther from it as soon as I caught up with him.

"Mahalo," I said, which was roughly a quarter of my Hawaiian vocabulary. Then I put the license away, picked up the keys and the rental agreement, and walked around the end of the long, narrow structure designed to keep the rental counters dry when the rain returned. I was greeted on the other side by another employee, who led me around my car in search of dings caused by previous drivers. When we were done, he held the door open for me while I climbed inside.

"Can you point me toward the Civic Auditorium?" I asked.

"You pointed at it now," he said. "Turn right you get to Manono; no can miss da kine."

"It's not far, then?"

"Not," he said. "But you *way* early, brah."

"So you know about the show?"

"Oh, yeah. I love dat fifties music."

So did I. But I had no interest in the Coasters, the Platters, or the Drifters that day—no matter who Danny might have flown in to perform under those names. And I was even earlier than my new friend could have guessed. I wasn't going to the show; I was going to the auditorium to wait for Danny to skate out the door with the gate receipts about halfway through the show.

That's when the weather was going to change, so my first step was to get my hands on a rainmaker. I started out following the directions to the auditorium, but I didn't stick with them very long. I turned left at the first traffic light, then left again just past the Borders bookstore a few minutes later. I could see a Wal-Mart off to my left and a sprawling mall to my right, which matched the instructions on the slip of paper in the pocket of my aloha shirt. I drove between those landmarks briefly, and then I pulled into a KFC parking lot and stopped.

That put me at the right place at the wrong time. I climbed out of the car and walked back to the Borders store; there are more weapons for killing time in a bookstore than anywhere else on earth, and this one was no exception. The place was jammed, but it had no problem absorbing one more browser.

I drifted over to the mystery section and walked up the alphabet to *V*, which is where I found the book I was looking for in the hands of the woman with the scar on her face. The scar was thin and pale and ran from just below her left ear almost to the point of her chin, and I was drawn to stare at it even though the face it traversed was itself worth extended viewing.

I moved my eyes to the shelf in front of the woman long enough to confirm that she was holding the only copy of the book in sight, then I let my eyes go wherever they desired. She mixed truly stunning beauty with tangible physical strength in a way I had never encountered before, as though she had come to that spot from the cover of a glamour magazine by way of a Universal weight machine—except that her muscles didn't bulge, they rippled, like she had developed them for actual use rather than display.

I was two or three feet away from the woman, but the way she inhabited the space she was in made me feel much closer than that. She was almost six feet long, most of that distance sticking out of the simple shift she was wearing in one direction or another. Everything the shift revealed was brown and muscled except her hair, which was black and damp and hung almost to her waist. The hair rippled with a beauty all its own when she tossed her head, which she did just before she turned to look at me observing her.

"Am I in your way?" she asked quietly, her eyes conducting her own inventory while she waited for my response.

"No," I said. I started to say something more, but stopped before the word had any air in it. The woman noticed my false start and responded to it.

"What?" she asked.

"I was going to say 'unfortunately,'" I said.

Her dark eyes were deep and apparently could see things; when she trained them on me, I felt thoroughly observed. "Go ahead," she said after she had seen enough.

"Unfortunately," I said, and a grin flashed across those eyes for an instant after I said it. I was encouraged by that response, so I said something else. "Have you read him before?"

"Everything he's written but this, I think," she said, raising the book in her hands briefly.

"Kind of rough reading," I said.

"Yes," she said.

"Do you know what draws you to him?"

"Yes," she said again, and then she brought the grin back to her eyes while she watched me figure out that I had asked the wrong question.

"What draws you to him?" I asked through a grin of my own.

"All of his repeating characters are wounded somehow, but they all keep coming back. I like that."

I nodded slowly, thinking I knew exactly what she meant even though I don't have a scar across the side of my face. "I saw him speak once," I said.

"Really? I didn't know he was here."

"This wasn't here. It was where I'm from in Oregon."

"You look more like you're from here than Oregon."

"Well, I guess I am. But that was before I was born."

This time she was the one who nodded slowly. I stood there next to her and watched her do it until she spoke again. "What was he like?" she asked.

"Who?"

"Him," she said, the grin in her eyes finally spreading across her face.

"Oh, yeah," I said. "He was brutal."

"What do you mean?"

"He ripped the throat out of a suburban housewife who kept asking him to congratulate her for starting a Stranger Danger program to protect the local kids from sexual predators."

"He didn't think strangers were the crux of the problem?"

"No, he didn't."

"He's right about that," she said, and the grin vanished from everywhere while she said it.

"I know," I said. "The woman was asking for it, but that didn't make it any easier to watch."

"Kind of like his books?"

"Exactly," I said.

"What draws *you* to him?"

"All of his repeating characters are wounded somehow, but they keep coming back. I like that."

"Are you mocking me?"

"No."

"Are you wounded, then?"

"Profoundly," I said, staring briefly at the scar I had actually forgotten for a while. She watched this transpire before she spoke again.

"You aren't going to ask about the scar, are you?"

"No," I said.

"Are you too polite or too afraid?"

"I see it as more of a need-to-know kind of thing."

"What does that mean?"

"When I need to know," I said, "you'll tell me."

"That's pretty good," she said, and then we both got our grins back and stood there for a moment while we used them.

"I take it you were looking for this book, too," she said, holding up the book in her hands.

"Yeah," I said.

"I'm going to buy it," she said. "If you look me up when I finish with it, I'll loan it to you."

"I'm afraid I won't be here that long," I said.

"It won't take me long," she said. "Plus you can always decide to come back if you have to leave too soon. Right?"

"Right," I said, after I thought about it for a moment. "I'll keep that in mind."

"Do," she said. Then she moved past me and walked to the end of the aisle exactly as I had thought she would move, her lethal legs doing one job and her hips doing another, and I stood there breathing in the trace of her fragrance and watched until she was gone.

T W O

When the afternoon was finally dead, I walked back to my car, hit the trunk release, leaned against the door on the driver's side, and started waiting again.

The sun was dropping out of the sky more rapidly than I was used to, and I watched the night descend on the town and everyone in it. Clouds were scuttling in, too, and the air became denser around me.

The rain started a few minutes later, soft and warm where it touched my skin. I stayed in my spot against the car and let it fall. After a moment or two, a car door opened about twenty yards from me and a thick, dark man climbed out. He was shorter than my five ten but twice as wide, and the only thing I could see popping out of the shorts and tank top he was wearing was muscle.

He was carrying a small gym bag in his right hand as he approached me, and when he got to my car he dropped the bag into my trunk and slammed the lid.

"Can that be traced back to you?" I asked.

"Nah," he said. "No way. But one t'ing—you got only fo' rounds."

I raised my eyebrows slightly in response to this information, but he shrugged. "Dat's da way it come," he said.

"Four rounds is plenty," I said. "Thanks."

"No problem. Just tell Nofo I take care of you if he ask."

"I will."

"How you know dat moddafuckah?"

"He gave me a ride from Vegas to L.A. a while back," I said, remembering the trip I had made in Nofo's taxi with a friend the previous year—back when the friend was still alive. "I don't really know him that well," I added.

"Well, he know you, brah, or he no gimme da call."

"I guess we made a connection."

"No sheet," he said, his voice stretching it out a little and his eyes regarding me pensively for a moment. I felt like he was going to say something more, so I stood in the gentle rain and waited for him to spit it out.

"No shoot Samoan-kine security," he said finally. "I gonna be pissed I get one cousin shot."

"Tell all your cousins not to stand in front of a bullet," I said.

"Dis moddafuckah got da kine, you wanna let it ride, brah."

"If things get out of hand like that," I said, "I don't think I'll give a fuck how much Samoan security he has."

"You gonna give a fuck aftah, I get one cousin shot."

"No," I said quietly, "I won't. That's what I want you to understand."

I was still leaning against the door of the car and he was still standing next to the trunk, but the space between us seemed to shrink as we eyed each other through the rain. "Could put you down right heah, brah," he said when he had seen enough. "No gotta worry no mo'."

"That's what happens," I said with a shrug, "I won't have any worries, either. But things go down like that, the wrong guy walks."

"Why I care?"

"You care," I said, "and so do your cousins. I'm thinkin' we've all seen enough things go wrong."

I stopped talking after that, and so did he. I stopped look-ing at him, too, and started staring at the side of the Wal-Mart building across the street. After a while, I reached into my shirt pocket and removed the slip of paper with the in-structions for finding the spot we were sharing.

"You got a light?" I asked.

He pulled a Bic out of a pocket in his shorts and flipped it in my direction. I caught it in my right hand, set it on fire with one flick of my finger, and then put the flame to the corner of the paper. The paper flared quickly, even in the rain, and I dropped it on the damp pavement as soon as the flame threat-ened my hand.

"Thanks for the piece," I said as I extinguished the Bic and tossed it back. Then I opened the door of the car and slid be-hind the driver's wheel. I picked him up in my rearview mir-ror while I hit the button that opened the window in my door. I froze for a moment when I saw him drop the lighter into his pocket and reach behind his back, but his hand came out with a cell phone in it and he began to walk away.

I turned the key in the ignition, put the car in gear, and backtracked to the traffic light where the road coming out of the airport crossed the highway. I drove maybe five blocks, turned right, and drove maybe five more blocks to a big com-plex I couldn't miss on my right.

I could hear music pouring out of a concrete building as I turned into a parking lot choked with cars. I drifted away from the building until I found an empty slot, and then I parked and shut the car down. I was facing the side of the au-ditorium, but I started to lose sight of it as soon as the wipers went off and the rain began to pile up on the windshield.

I settled back to wait, slipping easily into the same space I used while making a living at a poker table. Traces of rain laced with music splashed through my open window, but one seemed like a small price to pay for the other. I leaned back in the damp air and lost myself in thoughts about the life and death stretched out behind me, and then about the life and death still to come.

Finally, I focused on Danny Alexander—and the way he started our journey to the strange and foreign land the father I had never known had once called home.

THREE

Danny Alexander had been Mickey Rooney or maybe even Judy Garland in a previous life—or maybe any kid in any movie who ever said, "Let's put on a show"—which is why he was there in Leon's office in La Center.

You wouldn't have known it at first glance, though, because first he wanted to demonstrate a card trick. "Pick a card, any card," Danny said, spreading a deck across Leon's tidy desk.

I have a low tolerance for card tricks. Cards play enough tricks on a Texas Hold'em pro without any help from wannabe magicians.

"Danny," I said, "we've seen all these before."

"This is a new one," he said. "Come on, pick a card."

"Leon," I said, "please tell Danny there hasn't been a new card trick for a century or so."

"There hasn't been a new card trick for a century or so," Leon said from behind the desk, his voice lower and thicker than Danny's or mine.

"Pick a card," Danny said again. "Any card."

"You better humor him," Leon said through the slimmest of grins. "We might never get rid of him otherwise."

"Fine," I said. I picked a card.

"Look at it," Danny said, "but don't let me see it."

I looked at it; I was holding the ace of spades. "Now what?" I asked.

"Now I read it," he said. "You're holding the ace of spades, right?"

I looked at Leon and showed him the card, and his eyebrows arched slightly when he looked back at me.

"What is this, a trick deck?" I said. I flipped the deck over on the desk and revealed that all of the cards were aces of spades. "Like I said, we've seen all this before."

"No," he said. "That's not the trick. Put the card on the desk."

"Fine," I said. I put the card on the desk, and Danny produced a shiny red cloth that resembled a handkerchief—except no one would ever blow his nose on material that fine. He showed me both sides of the material with a flourish.

"Nothing on either side," he said, and then he laid it carefully over my card. "This is the magical part. Ready?"

"Please," I said.

"*Abracadabra,*" he said, and then he removed the cloth with another flourish a lot like the first one. "Now, how much do you want to bet that I can guess what that card is before you can?"

I looked at Danny blankly before I said anything, and I thought for a while, too. Even though I can usually make my living playing poker, I don't like gambling at all. I stared at the card on the desk and then at Danny again, until I finished calculating that a wager in this case could be a dead-certain cinch if I set it up right.

"I get to go first?" I asked.

"Absolutely."

"You're on," I said.

"Seriously?"

"Any amount you say."

"I'll put a grand down that I can guess what that card is before you can."

"Do you have that much on you?"

"Sure."

"Let's see it," I said as I drew ten hundred-dollar bills out of my front left pocket and set them on the desk next to the card. I usually had about that many hundreds in that pocket whenever I sat down at a card table to work, but any more than that and I would have had to get it from Leon.

It turned out that Danny had more than a thousand dollars in his pocket, but he counted out a grand and stacked it next to mine.

"Beautiful," Danny said. "After you."

"The ace of spades," I said.

"Take a look," he said, "but don't let me see it." I picked up the card, but it wasn't the ace of spades.

"Put both of your hands on it," Danny said. "I'm having trouble picking up your vibe."

"What does my vibe have to do with it?"

"Whose trick is this, yours or mine?"

"Fine," I said, and I put both of my hands on the card.

He stood there for a moment, a grin that looked very good on him spreading across his handsome white face. "Oh," he said finally. "That's the ace of hearts."

I dropped the card faceup on the desk; it *was* the ace of hearts. "That's pretty damned incredible, Danny," I said as I picked up the money. "I didn't see you switch it at all."

"Hey!" he said. "*I* guessed it first."

"Right," I said. "That's what I bet on, wasn't it? You'd guess what the card was before I did?"

"You know perfectly well what I meant, Wiley."

"Yeah," I said. "But I know what you actually said, too."

"I thought this was a *business* meeting," he said. The blue eyes that had been dancing in front of me only a heartbeat earlier had suddenly clouded. "I don't know what you're doing here, anyway."

"I'm taking care of business, just like you guys, only I'm making more money than you guys are."

"Very funny," Danny said.

"What *are* you lookin' for here?" Leon said quietly, and by the time the question mark was out of his mouth their business meeting had officially begun.

"I've got John Lee Hooker coming at the end of the month," Danny said, still glaring at me. "I'd like Genevieve to open that show."

Meaning Genevieve James, the white blues singer who had become Leon's major project now that he was totally out of the sex industry. Now all he had to keep himself busy was Genevieve's career—not counting the casino in La Center, of course, or half of all the rental houses in northeast Portland.

"Why?" Leon said. "That show's gonna sell out anyway, right?"

"Most likely," Danny said, turning his attention to Leon and revving up an engine inside of himself somewhere. "But the gig would be *great* for Genevieve."

"Why do *you* care about that?"

"I always try to promote our local talent, Leon. You know that. I think she's as great as you do."

"Cut to the chase, Danny."

"Look, I can help you big time with what you're trying to do with her. She opens for John Lee, then maybe a few others, and then we get her hooked up to open for someone nationwide. Next thing you know, *she's* the headliner. She has that kind of talent, you know she does. All she needs is the exposure."

"Actually, she needs a lot more than that."

"What do you mean?"

"She needs a record deal, for one thing. Without that, a nationwide tour is kind of premature, don't you think?"

"Sure, that goes without saying. But there again, I can help. I've got the contacts, Leon, you know I do."

"And you want what for all this help, Danny?"

"A ticket to ride, that's all. She's gonna have a long run. Nobody has a longer shelf life than blues singers."

"I think you're right, Danny. The part I'm not too sure about is why we need you."

"I can grease the wheels, Leon. You're gonna get her there, sure, but she'll get there even sooner with me in the picture."

"I'm not in any particular hurry. She has a lot of time in front of her."

"That's something you never really know, though. Time is never guaranteed."

"True," Leon said. "But if she's not gonna be around for long, what's the point of all the hurry?"

"Geez, Leon, think about it, will you?"

"Nobody I deal with says 'geez,' Danny."

"Well, fuckin' think about it, then," Danny said.

"There you go," Leon said through his broadest grin of the day. "I *will* think about it, Danny. How soon do you need to know about the Hooker show?"

"Yesterday. But there's always another show if you need more time."

"How about tomorrow?"

"Tomorrow's great."

"Anything else?"

"That's it," Danny said. "Except now I have to go out in the cardroom and win back the grand Wiley just stole from me."

"You were gonna do that anyway, right?" Leon said as he rose from his seat behind the desk and began to walk Danny to the door.

"True," Danny said with a quick grin. "Take a serious look at this, Leon. It's a win-win situation, I swear it is."

"I appreciate the offer, Danny. You've got my attention."

"Thanks," Danny said, and then he left the room. Leon closed the door behind him and looked back at me without a word for a while.

"Doesn't he have a show tonight, too?" I asked.

"B. B. King," Leon said.

"You goin'?"

"Absolutely. I've never seen a bad B. B. King show."

"Same here," I said, but I noticed as we tossed these words back and forth that his eyes were not involved in the conversation.

"What?" I said.

"You ever see a win-win situation?" he said, still leaning easily against his door.

"Life looks more like a zero-sum game to me," I said. "Every time I win out there, *someone* loses."

"And vice versa," Leon said slowly, summing up a lot of rough history for both of us with that one expression. "How long have we known Danny?"

"Seems like forever," I said. "Assuming that we do know him. I didn't know he could do card tricks, for example."

"Didn't take you long to profit from that information, though," he said.

"I try to be careful with words," I said. "I used to teach the English language, remember?"

"And several other things, the way I remember it."

"Don't even go there, Leon."

"I didn't bring it up, bro'. You did."

"Well, now I'm dropping it," I said. I got up and joined him at his office door. "That shit is over."

"Mrs. Boomer doesn't seem to think so."

"Believe me, you're gonna work for her before I ever do it again."

"I'm not a teacher, Wiley."

"Neither am I," I said as I opened the office door. "About Danny, he did say something that bothered me a little."

"What's that?" Leon asked, looking down on my five-ten from his six-three exactly like he had been doing it since our days in the same high school where the inimitable Mrs. Boomer now served as principal.

"He seems to think he can win the grand back," I said, nodding slightly in the direction of the cardroom.

"So?"

"So I'd say his link to reality is a little loose. For your sake, I hope he knows the music business better than he knows poker."

"He knows the music business just fine," Leon said quietly, his eyes locked on something a lot farther away than his cardroom. "Did you know he gave the kid a job last month?"

"Ronnie?"

"Yeah. It's only part-time, but the kid loves it. He's prob'ly as good with all the shit behind the scenes as he is on the stage."

"That's sayin' somethin'. Not many people can do what Ronnie does on the stage."

"Yeah," Leon said, still pensive, still locked on something I couldn't see from my vantage point right next to him.

"Something wrong with that?" I asked.

"With the kid, no. With Danny, I'm not so sure."

"Seems like a nice thing to do," I said, "and Danny's always seemed like a nice enough guy."

"True," Leon said. "But things ain't always what they seem to be, are they?" Then we both filed out of his office, and neither of us said anything for a while.

FOUR

He's not gonna go for it, Danny said to himself as he made his way from Leon's office to the chip booth. *It was worth a shot, but I didn't really think he'd go for it.*

Not that it was a problem, really, because he wasn't actually interested in a piece of Genevieve James. He wanted the whole enchilada, and he knew there were several ways to get it. He already had his hooks into the nigger kid, and that would no doubt turn into something. Meanwhile, time was definitely on his side.

Watch and wait, he said silently. *All I have to do is watch and wait—and recognize the best way to skin this particular cat when I see it.*

Meanwhile, he had a couple of hours he could spare to make back some of the grand Wiley had just ripped off. *As long as I've been coming out here,* he thought, *I'm still on the outside looking in. It's gonna be so sweet when I finally get on top of these guys.*

He traded his remaining cash for chips, sat down at a three-six game, and got up two hours later, his time and his chips disappearing on exactly the same schedule for a change.

FIVE

"Let's take it from the bridge, fellas," the kid said, and the fellas took it from the bridge, the horns Leon was adding for the festival gig punching up the arrangement exactly like the kid had written it.

The kid laid down a funky groove, of course, working his electric bass like it was a living thing, and he had the others in the palm of his hand everywhere he went—the drummer who had always been solid well beyond that level now, the rhythm guitarist who had always been exceptional now at least a step beyond that.

Not to mention the lead guitarist, who I believed was now the best in the city even though he didn't yet have the name to go with his game. These guys all had two or three times as much experience as the kid, but all of them followed his lead like it was the most natural thing in the world.

So did Genevieve, who had her name on the whole thing and all of her hopes for the future tied up in it. She was a rookie just like the kid, but she unleashed her smoky vocals wherever the kid pointed them and never failed to tattoo the target dead center.

None of the above was what amazed me about the kid, though; the amazing thing was that Leon followed his lead just like everybody else. For better or for worse, Leon had never been a follower in his life. Even on the way to our state basketball championship in high school, when I was the one with the ball in my hands, he was still the one who pointed the way. He just went wherever his instincts indicated, and all I did was make sure the ball was there when he needed it.

Leon never followed for the same reason most leaders hesitate to do it: He believed he had more game than anyone else, so who would he follow? That was exactly how the kid got Leon in line, because everyone could see from the first day the kid walked in that he had more game than anyone in the room.

Which everyone could still see today, including me, who was only there because we were all going to the B. B. King show when the rehearsal ended. I know nothing about music except what it sounds like when it's good, and that is what Genevieve's band was sounding like again, the new horns pitching in as if they had been there all along. In the kid's fertile mind, they probably always had been.

"Ronnie's fuckin' unbelievable," I said between songs.

"That's what I thought at first," Leon said.

"What do you mean?"

"I'm a believer now."

Ronnie wandered over with a bottle of water in his hand. "Whatcha think, boss?" he said with his trademark grin all over his black face.

"Whatcha think I think?" Leon asked.

"I think you think we're ready."

"You think right, Ronnie."

"Wiley," the kid said to me. "How's it goin'?"

"I'm always good when you guys are doin' this thing," I said.

"That's what it's all about, you know? I'm glad you like it."

"I really do."

"You guys got your tickets for the show tonight?" he asked, and Leon answered with a nod.

"That's good," he said. "I think we've sold 'em all."

"With the festival cranking up tomorrow, you'd think tonight would be a bad day for more blues," I said.

"B. B.'s a monster," the kid said. "There's nobody in his class, really. You're gonna see a who's who of blues in the audience tonight."

"Like you guys," I said.

"Exactly," he said, his face lighting up with a smile. "Everybody who's anybody, *and* everybody who ain't."

"You're kind of a monster yourself, Ronnie."

"A baby monster, maybe," he said, "but thanks. You couldn't say a nicer thing to a guy like me."

"There ain't no guys like you," I said, "but you're welcome."

"See you tonight," he said, and then he went back to work and we went back to watching him do it.

S I X

The kid walked in at seven on the dot, which was the usual thing with this kid, but he had a look in his eye that Danny hadn't seen before and didn't much like.

"Hey," Danny said, but he was thinking this: *It's a good thing you play music instead of poker, kid.*

"Hey," the kid replied.

"How'd you like the show?" Danny asked, already knowing the answer. The kid had lapped it up all night like a junkie in a cutting room.

"Hot," the kid said, and that look in his eye dimmed for a moment while his mind wandered back to the previous night. "B. B. is the absolute shit. My hat is permanently off to that motherfucker."

"That he is," Danny said, but he saw the look creep back into the kid's eyes while he said it. "I've never seen a bad B. B. King show."

"I can believe it," the kid said, and Danny wanted him to stop right there, but the kid only paused for a count or two, then kept right on going. "Actually, there was something about last night that I wanted to ask you," he said.

"What's that?" Danny said, his gut starting to clench involuntarily.

"I think there was something funny going on with the show. It didn't quite square."

"What do you mean?"

"I was wondering why my count of the crowd seemed higher than the official ticket sales."

"You mean above and beyond the comps and whatevers?"

"Way above."

"Like how far?" Danny asked, although he knew the exact number.

"Couple hundred, minimum," Ronnie said.

"Wow," Danny said, but he was thinking this: *Right in the ballpark, kid—it was 223.* "What do you figure it means?" he said. "We have that many crashers?"

"With Lester on the door?" the kid said. "I don't think so."

Lester being three hundred pounds of muscle, lard, and nasty attitude, Danny thought, *I'd have to agree with you there.*

"What, then?" Danny asked, his intestines now twisted beyond all recognition.

"Well, that's what I wanted to ask you about. I can't come up with many possibilities."

The kid paused to stare at Danny for a moment, and Danny sat behind his desk with a steel fist closed tight in his gut and stared back.

"Could someone have slipped some counterfeit tickets in on us?" the kid asked finally.

Indeed someone could, Danny said to himself. *But I really wish we didn't have to go there, kid.* "You've got a good head on your shoulders, Ronnie," he said aloud, trying his best to project a tone of confidence that he didn't feel at all. "That is some very solid thinking. What you need to do now, though, is think a little bit more."

"I'm not sure what you mean."

"Who could really do something like this, you get right down to it?"

"You could," Ronnie said softly, the same look that had bugged Danny from the get-go spreading out of the kid's eyes now and messing up his entire face.

"That's right," Danny said quickly. "But I'm not sure you're looking at it right."

"I don't see that I have many choices," the kid said. "You're rippin' off the performers."

"Yes and no," Danny said, spinning as hard and fast as he could. "If I don't front the show, nobody makes a dime here, Ronnie. This way, they get enough to make it worth their while, I get enough to make it worth mine. Nobody gets hurt but the tax man."

"I don't look at it that way," Ronnie said. "I was B. B., I'd say you took money right out of my pocket."

"B. B.'s fine with it, though. He got what he *thought* was his. If he lives long enough, he'll be back next year to do it all again. What you *should* be thinking about instead of all this is why I gave you this gig in the first place."

"That question did cross my mind."

"What'd you come up with for an answer?"

"I'm still workin' on it."

"Let me help you out, then," Danny said, going for deep sincerity with all his heart. "I need someone who isn't asleep at the wheel. You see what I'm working with here—I have the original Neanderthal in Lester, and I have a guy with his panties twisted too tight to be worth a damn in James. I figure you're a bright young kid in the business, you have a gig with the next act that's going to bust out around here, and you might have enough sense to come in out of the rain when you can."

"That's what this thing is? Comin' in out of the rain?"

"That's *all* it is. It's nothing but common sense, really."

"There could be another way of lookin' at why you offered me this gig."

You bet your black butt, Danny thought. *You* are *a smart one, aren't you?* "What would that be?" he asked.

"You might just be lookin' down the road a little. Now that Leon's got Genevieve rollin', what's to stop him from movin' in on you? What if he starts thinkin' he can promote a show just as well as you can?"

"What would that have to do with you?"

"Maybe I'm just your window for keepin' an eye on him."

"Leon doesn't exactly fly under the radar, Ronnie. He's not that hard to watch. Plus we go back a while. He's not going to think like that."

"Maybe it's more the other way around. Maybe *you're* thinkin' about movin' into talent management."

"So you can see *me* stabbing an old friend in the back," Danny said, but what he thought was this: *"Maybe" falls a long way short of describing the situation, kid.*

"Like I said, I'm still workin' on it."

"I can't say that doesn't disappoint me, Ronnie, but that's a little off to the side of the point."

"And the point would be?"

"Do you or do you not have enough sense to come in out of the rain when you can?"

"I guess not."

"I'm sorry to hear that," Danny said, which he believed might have been the five most sincere words he had ever spoken in a row.

"Yeah," the kid said.

"So what happens next?" Danny asked, the icy fist pulling his innards perilously close to his throat.

"You know what has to happen next."

I guess I do, Danny whispered into his inner ear. *You aren't leaving me much of a choice, are you?* He got up from his office chair and walked around his desk, although his legs suddenly seemed to be constructed of rubber rather than bone and he had a hard time keeping his feet synchronized. "Go ahead and do what you have to do," he said where Ronnie could hear it.

Ronnie shrugged and turned in the direction of the office door. Danny took a good look at him from behind as some working room opened up between them—a slim brown kid with music pouring out of him even while he walked, a kid the ladies loved, a kid unfortunately as straight as that goddamned Mother Teresa. When Ronnie was the perfect distance away, Danny picked up a microphone stand from the assortment stacked next to the desk and hammered the back of the kid's head.

Ronnie dropped like every bone in his body had suddenly turned to soup. Danny's head was throbbing, and his eyes had to cut through a filmy red haze to see anything. He moved a step closer and teed off one more time, carving a downward arc through the air until the stand smashed into the kid's skull again.

Danny ran out of air after that, and for a moment or two he couldn't access a new supply. The moment or two passed, however, and so did the throbbing in his head and the red haze in front of his eyes.

"You'd think a nigger bass player would have enough rhythm to keep in step," he said as he dropped the microphone on top of the body on his floor. "What a wasted opportunity."

He moved back to his desk and leaned over his phone for a moment, breathing laboriously until the knot in his gut unraveled a little. Then he punched in enough numbers in the phone to start it ringing at the far end of the line.

"Pick up Lester and bring him to the office," he said when James put the ringing to rest.

"Why?" James asked.

"Dammit, James!" he shouted into the phone. "Would you please just do what the fuck I'm paying you to do?" Then he slammed the phone down, slumped into his chair, propped his weary head on his hands, and waited for his faggot and his ape to arrive.

SEVEN

I think of my life in terms of the deaths that occur—and in terms of those that do not—and I still believe there are too many of both.

I deserve to die, and occasionally I even desire that fate, but death just spits in my face and moves on to others much less deserving. That's why I have no respect for death at all—nothing that capricious warrants respect.

Not that death doesn't kick your ass. It sure as hell kicked mine the instant it descended on my daughter. But once you know that death does whatever the fuck it wants to do, there is little to be gained by giving it another thought.

Death's debris, however, is a horse in another race entirely. My daughter was never far from the front of my mind, and neither were all the people who fell in her wake while Leon and I chased down death's point man in that terrible episode. Then there were Miriam, who died before her time the following year, and Dookie, Miriam's pimp, who died *way* too late.

These were some of the ghosts on my mind that Independence Day. I was not alone on Julie's blanket, but even the most compelling of companions couldn't keep my mind free. The ghosts were always just below the surface, waiting for the slightest lull to sally from their shadows.

I was stretched out on my back with my eyes closed. The morning had threatened rain, but it was an idle threat that rolled off me like—well, like water. The blues work just as well for me rain or shine, so I was ready for the day's festivities no matter which way the weather turned.

The Fourth of July is party time in Portland, and the mother of all the parties is the blues festival in Waterfront Park. That's where I was, on the upper edge of the grassy bowl south of the Hawthorne Bridge. I could see the Willamette River rolling by in front of me whenever I opened my eyes, and whichever way I turned my head I could see a stage. The first show of the day was about fifteen minutes away on the bridge end of the bowl to my left, and that was the show we were all there to see. But in the lull while we were waiting, my mind wandered—and my ghosts came out to play.

"There goes a cute one," Alix said, gently bringing me back to the blanket. "Two o'clock."

I opened my eyes and looked off to my right where I thought two o'clock might be, and I was rewarded by the sight of a slight blonde in a pale blue tank top, white shorts, and sandals with a bit of heel beneath them. She was dressed for a different kind of day than the one we were in, so she was rubbing the goose bumps on her arms as she moved. Those weren't the only bumps I could see from my vantage point, but no one was rubbing the two poking enticingly against the thin fabric of the tank top.

I have no idea how women navigate in heels, but this one knew how to do it with a lot of room to spare. She had that roll in her stroll that makes guys like me and girls like Alix sit up straight. We watched her until she picked out a spot, and then the bronzed behemoth walking behind her got in the way and changed the whole experience.

"Very nice," Alix said softly.

"You're terrible," I said. "Don't you know it's not correct to objectify the feminine gender?"

"Not guilty," she said. "She obviously cares about her appearance—there's a lot of art in that picture, believe me. I'm just caring right along with her."

"Whatever," I said. "Guys get pummeled all the time for doing the same thing."

"It's not the same thing. Guys are pigs a lot of the time."

I wasn't sure I followed the first half of that statement, but I couldn't really argue with the second half, so I just ducked under the whole thing and turned my attention to Alix.

The blonde in blue had been very easy on the eyes, but she was nothing compared to Alix. I know, because that's the first thing I did after catching sight of her—I compared her to Alix. I did this all the time, and only one person I have ever seen came out of those comparisons favorably.

Alix was a lot like me; her family tree had roots on more than one continent. She was Vietnamese on one side, Scandinavian on the other, and gut-wrenching gorgeous all the way around. That's another thing I knew, because I had made that sweet round trip on many delightful occasions.

Still, her beauty was not the most striking thing about her. What caused most jaws to drop was the tight blonde curls spilling off the top of her beautiful head, because Alix was the first Vietnamese woman with natural blonde hair that most people had ever seen.

I was sprawled with my head in her lap, so I craned my neck back so I could look into her dark eyes. She peered at me effortlessly for a moment, and then she leaned down and kissed me softly on the forehead.

"You ready to head down to the stage?" she asked.

"Sure," I said, although I would have waited another ten minutes or so if I had been alone. I sat up and surveyed the crowd for a moment, and that's all it took to locate the kids. JJ and Scooter were chasing each other near the south stage to our right, and Quincy was careening after them as best he could. I glanced at Ronetta, who was sitting quietly to my left.

"Okay if we wander off?" I asked.

"I've got 'em," Ronetta said through the slightest hint of a grin.

"What's so funny?" I said, even though I already knew the answer.

"We are," she said. "But I like it like that."

She was right—we were kind of funny—but *I* liked it like that, too. There had only been three significant women in my life, and all three of them were in Waterfront Park that day: Alix, the one who loved me; Ronetta, the one I loved; and Julie, the one I married.

I looked back across the grass to the children in my life who were still alive. JJ and Scooter, the twins Ronetta had made with Leon rather than me, were thirteen that year; and Quincy, the son Alix had made with a man neither of us knew, was half of that.

Quincy suddenly tripped over a blade of grass—or his own two feet—and sprawled face first on the ground. He was too far away for the sound track to reach us, but I already knew that Quincy would suffer his misadventure in silence. I watched Scooter help him up, brush him off a little, and wave an all-clear in our direction; a moment later, all three of them were back in high gear.

I let my eyes wander back to Ronetta, something my eyes have been inclined to do since our middle-school days. Never in all those years had I been disappointed, and that day was no exception. But looking at Ronetta was a challenge, too, because she always looked back at me like she could read my mind—and found it mildly amusing.

That's the way she was looking at me from her perch on

Julie's blanket, but I didn't mind it at all. Her presence there was the first sign of spring after a long, cold winter between us, and I was basking in that tentative warmth.

She had taken the twins and stormed out of our lives almost two years earlier, immediately after Leon burned her house down around Sylvester the pimp. She had moved into my house in Forest Grove with Julie, and I hadn't seen any of them until they all came in for Genevieve's show at the festival that morning.

I had moved out on Julie long before Ronetta moved in, of course, and Julie and I eventually consummated our lingering divorce. In addition to the blanket, Julie had come to the festival with a new English prof from Pacific University. They had already wandered off arm in arm, him looking at her like he thought his glasses might melt.

"Is this guy okay?" I asked Ronetta.

"What guy?" she said softly, the grin glinting off the green in her eyes.

"You know who I'm talkin' about."

"Don't try to tell me you care, Wiley."

"I care," I said. "I wouldn't want her hooked up with a creep of some kind."

"Who knows?" she said. "Nobody ever knows about you guys."

"You know about me," I said simply.

"Yeah, but I've known you since the sixth grade."

"You knew about me at first sight."

"True," she said after she thought about it for a moment. "But you're not really a reoccurring phenomenon. Not in my experience, anyway."

"Nor in mine," Alix said from the opposite side of the blanket. She could have added *which we all know is extensive* but she didn't. What she added instead was "Unfortunately."

I looked from Ronetta to Alix and back again. I thought

about pinching myself to determine whether or not I was dreaming, but I decided against it because I knew exactly where I was.

"Don't give our spots to the first good-lookin' guy who comes by," I said as I rose and helped Alix to her feet.

"How 'bout the second?" Ronetta asked.

"Not him, either."

"I'll hold out just as long as I can," she said. "But no longer."

"No one can do more than that," I said. "Just keep in mind that looks are *way* overrated."

"Easy for you to say," Alix chimed in. "You're surrounded by the best-lookin' women here."

"That's why I know what I'm talkin' about," I said, although I had to duck a roundhouse right as soon as the words were out of my mouth. Then Alix and I began our journey to the front of the stage, where I began to discover that death was not done with me yet.

EIGHT

"Why do you have to go so soon?" she said from the doorway, the whine Danny hated already creeping into her voice.

"This isn't soon," Danny said as he studied his reflection in the bathroom mirror. "I've been here the entire night."

"The night doesn't start at four in the morning, Danny."

"It's almost noon now," Danny said. "That's an entire night, baby, believe me."

And if you don't believe me, Danny said silently to the golden boy staring out at him from the mirror, *then fuck you. Which I already did—and it wasn't anything special, girl. It most definitely wasn't special enough to listen to this damned whine.*

He bent close to the mirror to study his eyes, which were already more blue than red. *I'm going to be good as new before long*, he thought. *Maybe the worst of this nightmare is over.*

"It's not like this is one of *your* shows," she said, apparently oblivious to how *not* her whine was going over. "The festival can get along without you for a while."

Yes, Danny thought, *but can I get along without it? This is all about damage control now, baby. Once Leon gets his nose bent out of shape, he'll be about as easy to stop as a runaway train.*

"Damn, I look good!" Danny said aloud, and he watched

the golden boy in the mirror say exactly the same thing. "Isn't that right, girl?"

"Yeah," she said. "For whatever that's worth."

"What's that supposed to mean?"

"Looks are *way* overrated, Danny."

"That's where you're wrong, baby," Danny said. "I wouldn't be here at all if you didn't look every bit as good as you do."

"Is that supposed to be a compliment or what?" she asked, the whine kicking up another notch and the pout getting started on her lower lip. Danny hated the whine, but the pout always sexed her mouth up something serious. *Maybe I'm selling her a little short,* Danny said to himself. *Considering everything that went down before I got here, she did a heckuva job turning the night around.*

He turned away from the mirror and looked directly at her for the first time since he had left her bed—if he had been looking at her then. Her hair was tousled, but he liked that, and he liked the way her nipples stood up at the tips of her perfect breasts. *I'd love to put that pout to work,* he said to himself. *Maybe make that whine a hum. But a man has to take care of business if he wants the business to take care of him.*

"I can't lie to you," Danny said, even though they both knew that was a lie itself, and then he spoke the gospel truth. "You're always going to find me with a fine-looking woman, baby. But that's what you are, so it's all good. Right?"

She rode her answer through the doorway and didn't stop until her tits bumped into his chest. Then she put one hand on each side of his head and drew their lips together; and as soon as that was done, she made sure their tongues came together, too.

My oh my, Danny said to himself. *I'll be damned if she isn't getting to me again!* He thought about making a comment or two, but he swallowed whatever he was going to say as soon as he realized he'd have to end the kiss to speak.

Not that he gained much from his forbearance, since she broke off the kiss instead. "Are you sure you have to go?" she whined.

"I'm already gone, baby," Danny said, but by then he was actually regretting the fact. He walked around her, out of the bathroom, and across the living room to the sofa. He picked up his black leather jacket, tossed it casually over his shoulder, and moved easily to the outside door.

"I'll call you," he said. "See if you're up to another visit tonight. Really, you were great."

"Don't hold your breath, Danny. I've got better things to do than sit around here waiting for you to call."

"I won't stop breathing, I promise you, no matter how great you were," Danny said curtly, his mood suddenly turning sour again. "That's why there's more than one number in my phone." Then he let himself out of the apartment, closed the door on one last glimpse of her pouting in the bathroom doorway, and hustled down the short hall and outside to the Caddy waiting at the curb.

"James," he said as he settled into the front passenger seat, "are the guys you date as hard to hang out with as the women I date?"

"Don't get me started," James said. "It's fuckin' unbelievable."

"Why is that?" Danny asked as the car pulled out into the westbound traffic on Hawthorne.

"I said don't get me started," James said.

"I'd just like to know why every little thing with these drama queens is a bigger production than any show I've ever done."

James drove toward the river without another word.

What's your problem? Danny thought, but he didn't think it for long. He was focused fully on a more significant question long before the bridge rose up in front of them.

Keep your eyes on the prize, Dannyboy, he said silently. *It's all about damage control now.*

NINE

Leon was lounging to the left of the stage as we approached. I veered off in that direction while Alix drifted toward Julie and the professor to our right.

Leon always looked at ease, so that's how he looked that day. He was dressed in a thin turtleneck, slacks, dress shoes, and a short leather jacket, all exactly the same shade of brown. I knew his socks and his boxers were that same color, too, because Leon always dressed in only one color at a time—just like the guy in the John R. Tunis books I had told him about back when we were kids.

Leon *looked* at ease, but he was on edge. I could feel it before I even reached him. He seemed slightly taller than his actual height, and the rippling muscles always close beneath his chocolate-colored skin seemed more tightly coiled than usual.

"What's wrong?" I asked when I got close enough to be heard over the tuning of the instruments on the stage.

He looked down on me sleepily, one more clear indication of trouble. The edgier Leon felt, the less of his hooded brown eyes you could see.

"Ronnie's runnin' late," he said.

My eyes shifted to the stage instinctively, as though Leon might have simply overlooked the most charismatic bass player in town. But I didn't see Ronnie anywhere among the musicians and crew preparing for Genevieve's set. Nor did I see Genevieve, for that matter.

"Where's Gee?" I said.

"She's here," Leon said. "But she's not takin' it too well."

"The kid can't be the first musician to show up late on her," I said.

"How many times did *we* show up late for a ball game?" Leon asked, still looking at me through those slitted eyes.

"So he's like that," I said.

"Yeah," Leon said slowly. "He's like that."

"Can she do this thing without a bass player?"

"There's enough bass players in town right now to sink the fuckin' *Titanic*."

"There's only one Ronnie, though."

"True. But that's not really the problem."

I nodded and shifted my attention back to the stage. I didn't have to be told the problem, because we all felt the same way as Gee about the kid. He had taken over more than the band when he walked his chops and personality into our lives.

"How'd you get LeRoy here so fast?" I said, after a closer examination of the people on the stage revealed one of Portland's premier bass players tuning up where Ronnie should have been.

"That's the name of my game, bro'," Leon said softly. "That's what I'm doin' here."

I didn't have to be told that, either. Whatever Leon intended for his projects was always the way they turned out. Still, LeRoy's presence on the stage seemed to stretch the laws of physics.

"That's pretty damned fast," I said. "Even for you."

"He's a fan," Leon said with the slightest hint of a grin. "He was here to see the set."

"Makes sense to me," I said. "That's why we're all here."

Leon nodded slowly, and I felt his gaze shift over my shoulder until it could focus on the spot near the rim of the bowl that Ronetta was holding for us.

"How is she?" he asked.

"Good," I said. "It looks like the freeze is finally over."

"Can't really blame her for the freeze, though."

"No," I said, visions of Sylvester the pimp and his posse holding Ronetta and the kids at gunpoint flashing through my mind. "We sure as hell can't."

"If I can get this thing here cleared up, I think I could thoroughly enjoy this day."

"What's the next step?"

"I talk to Dannyboy," he said, which surprised me. Danny had contributed significantly to my income as a poker player over the years, thanks to his inability to actually learn how to play Texas Hold'em, but I couldn't immediately see why his name would come up in this conversation.

"What's Danny got to do with it?" I asked.

"According to Gee, they were 'sposed to be workin' together last night."

"I didn't know that," I said.

"I imagine there are lots of things you don't know," he said behind the slightest of grins.

"When will you be seein' him?" I asked.

"Unless I miss my guess," he said, and he looked at me like we both knew how often that ever happened, "he's on his way here right now."

"The sooner, the better," I said, which turned out to be just one more indication of how wrong a man who doesn't know everything can be.

TEN

"I hate baseball," Danny said into his phone as James pulled the car up to a festival entrance on Front Street. "I don't even understand the line. Don't you have anything else?"

"I've got the fight next week," Booker said into his ear. "But you don't like boxing, either."

"If I was in on the fix," Danny said as he climbed out of the car, "I'd like the fights just fine. It's being out of the damned loop that I don't like."

He stood in the crowd on the curb while James drove away, and when the light changed he moved across the street with everyone else. "So why'd you call?" Booker said. "I can't change the fuckin' season for you."

"I've got to get down on something. This hole between hoops and football is driving me nuts."

"Baseball or boxin', take your pick."

"What's the line on a knockout? There is no way that thing is going the distance."

Danny listened to the number while he flashed his pass at the gate. A redhead in a festival T-shirt and a grin waved him in, and he winked in her direction as he passed by. *Interesting, baby,* he said to himself, *but you aren't ever going to be interesting enough.*

"Give me five on that," he said into the phone.

"Five hundred on a knockout," Booker said.

"Right."

"You're on."

"And do something about July. They've stretched hoops all the way to June—why can't they squeeze July out of it, too?"

"Right. I'll call the fuckin' commissioner just as soon as you get off my phone."

"Thanks," Danny said. "I really appreciate that." He cut the connection and put the phone away. *Save the sarcasm*, he thought. *There is no legitimate excuse for July.*

He moved easily with the crowd until the north stage appeared on his left. *Showtime,* he said to himself as he veered across the grass toward the stage. *And I'm not talking about that fat white chick who's due to start singing in a minute.*

He almost ran into Leon and Wiley when he came around the corner of the stage. "Hey!" he said. "How's it hanging, fellas?"

"Hey, Danny," Wiley said quietly, but if Leon said anything it was a lot quieter than that because Danny didn't hear a thing come out of his mouth. What Leon did instead of talk was stand there and stare at him through a relentless pair of slitted eyes.

If you opened those, Danny thought, *you might see a hell of a lot better.* He kept that thought to himself while he looked over Leon's shoulder at the stage.

"I see you got LeRoy," he said after he thought he had looked up at the stage long enough. "That's a good pickup."

He could feel the heat go up in the space around the three of them, but he played it off for as long as he could. *Not yet,* he said to himself. *Let it build.*

Unfortunately, his guts started to roil again while he waited. When he couldn't stand it any longer, he looked at Wiley and Leon in quick succession. "I know he's not Ronnie," he said, "but he's damned good."

"You know where Ronnie is?" Leon asked softly.

"What? The kid didn't call?"

"We haven't heard shit," Leon said.

Not yet, Danny said to himself again. *Play it off a little longer.* "I know you're good, Leon," he said aloud. "But if the kid didn't call, how did you get LeRoy up there already?"

"You know where Ronnie is?" Leon asked again, as though Danny hadn't asked a question at all.

"All I know is what he said last night—something about a family emergency. I got the impression he was heading home."

"When did he leave your place?"

"I let him go early. Ten or ten-thirty, maybe."

"Where's home?" Wiley asked.

Danny and Leon looked at each other, but neither saw what he was looking for. "Did you ever hear him talk about that?" Danny asked.

"No," Leon said.

"Neither did I. If you judged it by his music, you'd say New Orleans or out in the cotton somewhere, but he didn't talk like any of that. I don't have a clue where he came here from."

"Maybe Genevieve knows," Wiley said.

"How's she taking it?" Danny asked.

"Hard," Leon said. "She doesn't think this is like him."

Now, Danny said to himself. *Dangle it out there a little.* "I wonder if I'm the one who messed up," he said aloud. "Maybe he thought I was going to call you guys."

"Why would he think that?" Leon said.

"Genevieve's right," Danny said. "This isn't like him at all. Maybe he just assumed I would relay the message."

"Maybe," Leon said.

"I'd apologize if it was my bad," Danny said with a grin. "But you couldn't have done better than LeRoy no matter when you found out."

"That's the truth," Leon said.

"I'm sure you'll hear from him soon. Meanwhile, I guess the show is still going on."

"Yeah," Leon said, his hooded eyes still barely visible and his soft voice only a click or two above a whisper. "The motherfuckin' show always goes on."

Tell me about it, Danny said to himself as they all turned their eyes toward the deejay stepping up to a microphone to introduce Genevieve and her band. *And it's going to take one sensational performance to keep all of these damned balls in the air.*

ELEVEN

The band was short of its usual snap, crackle, and pop, but Genevieve still soared through her set. She converted her concern for Ronnie into music and threw a mix down on us strong enough to stick for the rest of the day.

Leon and I lingered in front of the stage when she was done while Alix, Julie, and the professor drifted back to Ronetta and the blanket. The next set had begun on the stage at the opposite end of the bowl by the time Genevieve and Ebony joined us.

Genevieve lost a lover when I lost my daughter, but one of those is easier to replace than the other. Ebony eventually filled that empty place to overflowing for Gee, and I hardly ever held their good fortune against either of them. I had earned that hole in my life, after all, through the years of benign neglect—or worse—which had preceded Lizzie's death.

If you looked at either Ebony or Genevieve individually, you would never conjure up the other. Ebony was a lean assortment of hard black angles; Genevieve a generous accumulation of soft white folds. When they were together, though, the most cursory of glances revealed the electric connection between them.

"Thanks for bein' here," Genevieve said as she walked up and wrapped her arms around me. "I really appreciate it."

"My pleasure, Gee," I said.

"Were we bad?" she asked.

"No," I said. I hugged her back and kissed her softly on the top of her head, and then I lifted my eyes and nodded a silent hello at Ebony. That was the thing about Ebony—always off to the side somewhere, watching calmly and apparently at perfect peace while Gee soaked up all the attention available anywhere in the vicinity.

"Hey, Wiley," Ebony said with a quiet grin, as though she knew exactly what I was thinking.

"What are we gonna do?" Genevieve said, turning toward Leon. He looked at me, so I answered.

"You guys have your hands full today," I said. "Let me see what I can find out."

"Would you?" she asked. "I'm really worried about him."

"It's probably just an oversight," I said. "He told Danny he had a family emergency last night."

"It's something worse than that," she said with a soft catch in her smoky voice that caused me to look at her more closely. She was weeping quietly and apparently without effort, just standing there with the tears running down both sides of her face.

"It's something bad, Wiley," she added as soon as she could navigate the words through her silent tears. "I can feel it."

"I'll get right on it," I said. "Where does he stay?"

Genevieve's voice drowned for a moment when she tried to respond to that, but Ebony picked up the slack. "That's part of the problem," she said. "He's using our spare room, but he doesn't actually stay there much."

"Then how do I find his latest admirer?"

"That's the name of this game," Leon interjected. "The kid has more beds around this town than I ever did."

"Who was the last one you know about?"

"Someone named Jane," Leon said with a shrug. "A very leggy white girl."

"Just plain Jane?" I asked.

"She isn't plain," Ebony said. "Believe me."

"Go on up and say hi to Ronetta and the rest," I said. "Tell 'em I'll be tied up for a while."

"Thanks, Wiley," Genevieve managed to say as she kissed me on the cheek. "I mean it."

"We'll get it all sorted out pretty soon," I said, with the perfect certainty of total ignorance. "Try not to worry."

She smiled wanly, reached out her hand for Ebony, and started a slow climb to Julie's blanket. I watched them go, and Leon stood behind his slitted eyes and watched them with me.

"What the fuck is goin' on?" I asked.

"I'm with Genevieve on this one, bro'," he said quietly. "This feels like some serious shit to me."

"Go ahead," I said, nodding toward the mother of his children and the love of my life. "I'll keep you posted."

"Do that," he said, and he moved off easily in the general direction of Ronetta and the others. Meanwhile, I stood there like a statue of myself and watched them all make their way up the slope—the only one not moving, the only one completely clueless about where to go.

TWELVE

How am I doing so far? Danny said to himself as he watched Leon stride up the slope. *So far, so good?*

Leon made no discernible response, but Danny already knew the answer. "You bet your sweet butt I'm good," he mumbled softly.

"Don't I know it," someone said behind him. He turned and ran a practiced eye up and down a slim blonde in a blue tank top and white shorts standing a step or two away, and he smiled as he saw her doing exactly the same thing to him.

"Get away from me, girl," he said. "I'm too young to die."

"If I was lethal," she said through a smile of her own, "wouldn't you be dead already?"

"It isn't you, Sara Sue, it's that muscle-bound monstrosity you hang out with."

"He's nothin' but a little puppy. Why is everybody afraid of him?"

"The fact that he can break most people in half with his bare hands might have something to do with it."

"Oh, pooh," Sara Sue said. "Besides, he's not always around."

"Where is he right now?" Danny asked.

"He went to pee. You're safe for another minute or two, anyway."

"Go ahead and laugh. I don't think I have whatever you use to make a puppy out of him."

"No, you don't. But I like what you do have."

"So do I," Danny said. "That's why I don't want anything to happen to it."

"Call me tonight. He's gonna be out of town, scout's honor."

"What the hell kind of scout were you?" Danny asked, eyeballing one more time the delicious way her perky nipples pushed against her thin tank top.

"A *boy* scout, of course. That's why we're havin' this conversation."

"I just might do that, Sara Sue, but I have to be here until late."

"Believe me, Danny," she said, stepping close and drawing his left ear to her lips, "you can skip the fireworks show. Call me."

She stood like that for a moment, letting him inhale her once or twice, then she moved around him and began to climb the slope on a pair of heeled sandals. Danny watched the sleek roll of her hips and the way her long bare legs ran all the way from the edge of her shorts to the ground.

That is some dangerous stuff, he said to himself, *but what a way to go!* He grinned around that thought and the buzz in his genitals that came with it, and he rode smoothly on top of it all until he noticed Wiley moving up on him from the direction of the silent stage to his right.

THIRTEEN

Portland is full of people who can really blow. Lloyd Jones and his crackerjack band had drawn most of the people in the bowl to the south stage by the time I got my feet moving. Although the festival attracted some of the top names in blues every year, the local guns like Lloyd never suffered much by comparison.

It wasn't Lloyd's hot slide guitar that finally got me going, though; it was Danny and the blonde in the blue tank top. If you don't know where to go next, you might as well turn around and go back: If life truly is a circle, as some people believe, you should reach the same destination either way.

By the time I reached Danny, the blonde was rolling back up the slope. He was unabashedly savoring every step, but I kept my eyes locked on him until he turned to acknowledge my approach.

"Man oh man!" he said with a grin. "Is that Sara Sue sweet or what?"

"I think the guy she came in with is bigger than both of us put together," I said.

"And she's all the sweeter because of it, don't you think?"

"Not really," I said.

"Forbidden fruit is always sweeter, Wiley. Just like the grass really *is* always greener on the other side of the street."

"I'm from Oakland, Danny. The grass down there was dead on both sides of the street."

"Really? I didn't know that."

"It's not literally true. I was trying to be funny."

"I mean I always thought you were from Hawai'i."

"I get that a lot."

"So you're *not* Hawaiian?"

"My father was Hawaiian," I said. "Does that make me one, too?"

"I think so, yes."

"There you go, then. You were right all along."

"Have you ever been there?"

"No."

"I do a couple of shows over there every year. The place is truly paradise, Wiley, just like they say. You really should check it out."

"It's on my list of things to do, Danny. Maybe after I find out what's goin' on with Ronnie."

"I'm not sure what more I can do for you there."

"Do you know this woman he was hangin' out with? Jane something?"

"Jane Gottesman? Not as well as I'd like to, let me tell you. But that might be old news by now. I haven't seen her around lately, now that I think about it."

"You know where I can find her?"

"Up on Alameda, I think somewhere in the twenties."

I raised my eyebrows in response to that location, and Danny nodded in agreement. "I know," he said. "A very high-rent lady, believe me."

"What are my chances of going door to door until I find her?"

"Just stop when you get to a leggy brunette with a look in her eyes that will melt the buckle on your belt," he said through another grin. "If it's not her, it'll be someone just like her."

"Leon called her that, too."

"What?"

"Leggy. What the hell is that?"

"It means her legs run all the way from you know where to the ground, Wiley."

"Almost everyone's legs do that."

"*And* all the way back again. Trust me—everyone's legs *don't* do this. You'll know it when you see it."

"If you say so."

"Look, I have to run. Don't worry about Ronnie. He's going to call soon and clear this whole thing up."

"You're probably right," I said. "Thanks for the help, anyway."

"Like I said, the whole mix-up might be my fault." Then he tapped my left arm lightly and moved briskly toward the north stage, where the third act of the day was setting up. When he reached the corner where Leon and I had been standing during Genevieve's set, he walked around it and disappeared.

I stared in Danny's direction as he left, but I wasn't really looking at him. The only thing I could see was the vibrant face of a kid born to play music who had just missed the biggest showcase of his young life.

FOURTEEN

"So far, so good," Danny mumbled under his breath as he walked around the corner of the stage and out of Wiley's sight. "But I have a whole lot farther to go."

He stopped as soon as he saw Lester in the knot of people buzzing around the ramp to the stage, and after a moment or two Lester unraveled himself and walked his bald head across the distance between them.

"Do you have those tickets ready for next week?" Danny asked.

"When did I say I'd have 'em?" Lester said as he tried to mop the sweat pouring down his face with a towel draped around his massive shoulders.

"No later than Monday," Danny said.

"What day is this?"

"Saturday."

"Any other questions?"

Why do I put up with this fat fool? Danny thought, but he didn't have to look at Lester long to remember the answer to that question.

"When did you develop that smart mouth you've got on you?" Danny asked.

"Soon as I found out I can talk any way I fuckin' please."

"That would do it," Danny said.

"How'd it go with Leon?" Lester asked.

"It looks good so far," Danny said, "but I always have a little trouble reading that guy."

"Doesn't give you a lot to work with, does he?"

"No."

"Look," Lester said, "I'm workin' here."

"Hang on another second. I think we might need a diversion, just to be sure."

"Less is more with these guys," Lester said. "You'd be better off lettin' it ride if it's workin' the way it is."

"I don't know. Isn't it just a matter of time before they end up right back with me?"

"Maybe," Lester said, wiping the towel across his face again. "Ain't all that many places to look, are there?"

"That's what I'm saying. The right diversion might give them something more important to think about."

"Maybe," Lester said again. "But they see it's connected to you, it'll just make things worse."

"It has to be done so they don't see that."

"You don't benefit enough to justify the risk. Eventually, they'll work through the diversion and end up right back where we are now."

"Enough time goes by, maybe I can reshuffle the deck somehow."

"Where can you get a new shuffle in the middle of a hand?" Lester asked. "If you think you have to do something, it makes a lot more sense to hit the motherfuckers than to try to divert their attention."

"I've known them for a long time, Lester. I don't think I can do that."

"Maybe you shouldn't have clocked the kid, then."

"He didn't give me any choice."

"Neither will these guys, believe me. You said it yourself— it's only a matter of time."

"Well, we're not there yet. You give me the right diversion, maybe we'll never get there."

Lester started shaking his head slowly, and Danny stood there quietly and watched him do it. "What kind of a diversion you got in mind?" Lester said after a moment or two.

"The less I know about it, the better. Just make sure it doesn't point back to me."

"Wiley or Leon?"

"I don't think it matters. If you cut one of them, I think they both bleed."

"It's gonna cost you."

"How much?"

"You have to ask, you can't afford to do it."

"Whatever," Danny said. "Just give me a little room to breathe."

"I can do that," Lester said, and then he ambled back to the worker bees buzzing around the stage. Danny could feel the short blond hairs stand up on the back of his neck while he watched Lester go.

Geez, Danny thought. *What did I ever do to deserve this headache?*

FIFTEEN

I left the park as soon as Danny walked around the edge of the stage, but I had to swim against the tide of blues fans streaming through the gate to do it. I could see the sun on their faces, so I knew the early clouds were burning away somewhere above and behind me as I picked my way across Front Street and stepped into the long shadows of downtown Portland.

The first phone book I came to revealed a pair of Gottesmans, neither with the name Jane nor with an address affixed to it. One of them started with numbers I associated with the northeast part of town, so that's the one I dialed.

"Gottesmans'," someone said, and the someone could have been speaking from the far side of the Rio Grande if someone would ever have a reason to say "Gottesmans' " there.

"May I speak to Jane, please?" I said.

"The *señora* is not at home," the someone said. "May I take a message?"

"That depends on when she might get it," I said. "Do you know when she'll be back?"

"The party starts in less than an hour. She'll be back before then."

"That's what I'm calling about," I lied. "I have an order for the party ready, but I seem to have misplaced the address."

"Who is this?" the someone asked sharply. "I am expecting no such order."

I cut the connection, hung up the phone, and finished the short hike to the bus mall that flows through the center of town like a concrete river. *I should have known,* I said to myself as I walked. *Leggy ladies who like hot bass players don't have time to plan their own parties.*

I had to wait about twenty minutes for the number 33, and then I had to ride it for twenty minutes before it dropped me along the basketball courts at the northwest corner of Irving Park. The courts were busy, and I scanned the action absentmindedly while I walked the block up Fremont to Eighth.

The same courts had been in exactly the same place two decades earlier, when Leon and I had first crossed paths there as high school kids. We both saw our entire future together the first time we looked into each other's eyes—that I was born to get him the ball, and he was born to shoot it.

I had that moment in my head when Jesse saw me from the nearest court. He had the ball and was pushing it hard in my general direction when he suddenly jumped on the brakes.

"Hold it!" he said abruptly. Everybody on his court held it, most of them turning to see what he was looking at.

"You want some of this, old-timer?" he yelled, holding his thick brown arms straight out from his body while he palmed the ball in his big right hand.

"Still too soon, Jesse!" I hollered back. "I promised your mama I wouldn't whup you before you were a grown man!"

"Shit!" Jesse said through a grin almost as wide as the court he was standing on. "I didn't make *yo'* mama no fuckin' promises!"

I waved and continued on my way, even though I usually felt more at home within those clearly marked confines than in the house on Eighth where I parked my old Subaru and occasionally laid my weary self down to sleep.

The house on Eighth was the second smallest of Leon's many rental properties, but it was way too big for me. His smallest house had been a slightly better fit, but I quit living there after Leon blew up Tee the bodyguard's head in my face while I was sprawled on the kitchen floor with Tee's gun punching a hole in my forehead.

When I reached the house, I pushed the old shit out of my mind while I walked around to the back door and entered through the kitchen. I didn't stop until I reached the full-length mirror on the bedroom door, which I used to help me decide if I was dressed right for a Fourth of July party up on Alameda.

SIXTEEN

"Pick me up," Danny said into his phone.

"Where?" James asked.

"The same place you dropped me."

"Give me five minutes."

"Perfect," Danny said. He cut the connection and put the phone away. Five minutes later, he climbed into the passenger seat.

"You know," he said, "Lloyd Jones is just as good as anyone here."

"If you say so," James said flatly.

"I do, James. I do. It's actually unbelievable how deep we are around here, when you think about it."

James made no response to that except to unsnap his seat belt, open his door, climb out of the car, and toss a cell phone onto the seat he had just vacated.

"What are you doing?" Danny said.

James responded to that by slamming the car door shut and walking in front of the vehicle to the sidewalk. A horn started blasting from the car directly behind Danny, but he ignored it while he clambered out of his seat.

"What are you doing?" he said again as soon as he hit the sidewalk.

"I'm quitting," James said simply.

"Who said you can quit?" Danny said, his face getting redder and his voice louder while he said it.

"Abraham Lincoln," James said.

The horn blasted again. Danny held up one hand in the general direction of the car with the horn, but he kept his focus on James. "What are you talking about?" he said.

"I'm out of here," James said. "This shit you're into now is *way* over my head."

"There's no place you can go to get out from under it, you stupid idiot!"

"Sure there is," James said, and he turned and walked himself into the flow of fans moving toward the gate Danny had just passed through from the opposite direction.

"Hey, asshole!" someone shouted from the street. "Move that motherfuckin' piece of shit!"

Danny spun toward the street with a sharp retort on the tip of his tongue, but he peeled his voice off his comment as soon as he saw the size of the guy behind the shout. *Geez,* he said to himself as he slammed the passenger door and moved around to the driver's side. *How did that gorilla ever cram himself into that car?*

He threw the Caddy into gear and let it roll north on Front Street, but he had to dig the cell phone out from under his butt before he could do it. He crossed the river when Front forked at the Steel Bridge and then drifted along to the north.

Abraham Lincoln? he said without a sound. *Where did that come from?*

No one in the Caddy knew the answer to that question, so no one made a reply. But the scene back on Front Street kept running through Danny's head, and he asked the same question every time he got to the end of the loop.

That damned faggot is right about one thing, he thought as he slipped off the freeway. *This whole scenario is going to be too deep for all of us before much longer.*

Three or four minutes later, Danny parked the Caddy and walked through the door of Leon's casino. All five poker tables were in play, but one of them was short a player or two.

"Larry, my man!" Danny said to the guy counting out a deck of cards in the cashier's cubicle at the front of the cardroom.

"Hey," Larry said, but he didn't look up until he was done with the deck. "Didn't expect to see you today."

"Why not?" Danny asked. "You see me almost every day."

"I was in your shoes, my butt would be down by the river today."

If you were in my shoes, Danny said to himself, *you have no clue where you'd be today.* "If you were in my shoes," he said aloud, "you'd have the same responsibilities here that I have. You know I promised to teach these fools how to play this game."

"I'm not too sure they all wanna learn, Danny. We got some certified hardheads in here."

"Come on now, Larry," Danny said. "Where would someone get certified for something like that?"

"You want that three-six seat?" Larry said through a grin and a nod in the direction of the table with an open slot. "Or you wanna wait for something richer?"

"Low rent, high rent, what difference does it make? I have to teach them all, don't I?"

"Anything else would be discriminatory."

"Exactly," Danny said. He peeled a picture of Benjamin Franklin off the roll in his pocket and slapped it on the counter. Larry handed him a rack of chips and made the money disappear.

"And let the lessons begin!" Larry said, the grin even wider now than before.

Danny winked and walked over to the open seat. "Now pay attention!" he said as he spilled the chips onto the table. "I don't have the whole damned day to work with you fools."

"If that's all the chips you have," Leonard said from the

end of the table to Danny's right, "you don't have more than an hour or so."

"An hour from now, Leonard, I'll be playing with *your* chips. Now the rest of you fools, take some damned notes so you don't forget how I do it."

That put a grin on Leonard's lean lips, and everyone at the table either grinned along with him or laughed out loud. And they all did exactly the same thing forty-seven minutes later, when Danny briefly interrupted his lessons to swap Larry another Franklin for another rack of chips.

SEVENTEEN

I decided to walk in search of leggy Jane, even though the trek from Eighth and Fremont to somewhere in the twenties on Alameda was uphill all the way. I didn't give the slope a second thought—I am accustomed to uphill climbs. Every attempt I made to move out of the hole I had dug for myself involved a climb of one degree or another.

I started by stopping. Gee and Ebony shared another of Leon's houses about two blocks east of mine, and I climbed the steep driveway and then the stairs to the front porch as soon as I got there. I shivered slightly while I fumbled for the key behind the planter, even though the sun had burned through the cloud cover well enough to beam down unimpeded on the back of my neck.

I normally avoided this house, and the entire block of Tenth that ran in front of it. Nor would I have come within sight of it that day if it hadn't seemed imperative to examine Ronnie's room. I liked Genevieve, but her house would never be anything to me but the place my daughter had been living when she died.

The spare bedroom was off the living room at the front of the house, so I opened the front door with the key and turned to my right as soon as I walked inside. The door to Ronnie's room was open, so I kept on walking until I cleared that doorway as well. It was a small room that peeked out around an even smaller bed, and I saw almost nothing at first glance that suggested Ronnie had ever used either one.

The single exception was a framed photo of a teenaged Ronnie lodged happily between a man and a woman probably two or three times his age. I picked the photo off the top of a low chest of drawers and studied it for a moment. All three of the camera's subjects had been grinning like fools when the shutter clicked; all three of them looked like there was nowhere they would rather be. It was the kind of photo that made you want to crack the frame and jump inside.

I placed the photo back where I had found it as soon as I couldn't stand to look at it any longer. There was nothing else on top of the chest of drawers, and nothing on top of the small table next to the bed except a shadeless lamp. I found clothes stacked neatly inside the drawers and hanging just as neatly in a portable closet, but I found nothing that really rang of Ronnie or pointed me toward where he might have gone: no shaving gear, no luggage, no musical instruments, no address books, no discarded mail with return addresses in the upper left corners of the envelopes.

My feet were back on the sidewalk not more than five minutes after I had first veered up Gee's driveway, one moving after the other as if they knew exactly where they were going. I had hedged my bet by leaving the old Subaru behind: If I didn't find the right Fourth of July party by the time I walked from one end of the twenties to the other, I would at least have logged my workout for the day.

I started at the far end, a circuitous route forced on me by an ancient accident of nature. Alameda rides along a high ridge that the affluent use to look down on the rest of northeast Portland, so I needed the moves of a mountain goat to walk a straight line from Gee's house to leggy Jane's no matter where on Alameda Jane turned out to be.

I no longer had moves of that kind, so I went back to Fremont and headed east. I walked in and out of the sun all the way to Thirty-third because Fremont is lined with leafy trees in the summer, and then I turned north for another block or so.

Alameda meandered off to the northwest from there, so I meandered with it. I was looking for houses that seemed to have attracted an inordinate number of cars, and I found three before someone somewhere around Twenty-eighth offered an affirmative answer when I asked, "Is this the Gottesman residence?"

The someone was short and square. He was wearing walking shorts and a polo shirt that seemed to belong together, and everything that stuck out of the ensemble had the kind of tan on it that comes from running around in the sun with a tennis racket or a golf club in your hand. He squinted up at me briefly through a pair of horn-rimmed glasses and then stuck out his right hand.

"Indeed it is," he said. "I'm Jack."

"Wiley," I said as I grasped the hand sticking out at me. I was thinking that this must be one heckuva party if the host didn't even know all of the guests, but I didn't share that thought with Jack.

"Great to meet you," he said. "Jane's out back. Just head due south and you'll eventually run right into her." He stepped out of the doorway to usher me in, but his attention had already rotated to a couple coming up the walkway behind me.

I followed Jack's advice and headed due south, but what I eventually ran into was the rail on a huge cedar deck overlooking a sprawling backyard choked with people and a large slice of Portland beyond that. There was a bar set up to my right, and there was a long, slim tender set up behind the bar. There was no one in front of the bar but me, which

I found hard to understand until I checked out the yard again and found three more watering stations just like the one on the deck—only busier.

"Happy Independence Day," I said, turning back to the bartender with what I hoped was a light twist of irony.

"Can I get you anything?" he replied, with the slightest possible suggestion of a grin playing around the corners of his mouth as he spoke.

"Can you point me toward Mrs. Gottesman?"

"I can," he said, the grin growing all the way to a flicker, "but there's no need."

I raised my eyebrows slightly while I waited for additional information, but he said nothing more. Then I looked back over the rail and comprehended fully for the first time the concept of "leggy."

It has nothing to do with height. The thin woman I observed approaching the deck with a glass of ice in her hand was no taller than the man I had met at the front door. And it has only a rudimentary connection to that roll in the stroll Alix and I—and Dannyboy—had admired on the blonde at Waterfront Park that morning. This was that same stroll, maybe, but distilled into its basic essence and then mixed with something that nobody else knows anything about.

The woman's legs did appear to run all the way to the ground and back. I saw them flash occasionally through a slit on one side of a long, flowing dress that might actually have been a random piece of material she had snatched off the floor and knotted over one shoulder when the doorbell rang to announce the arrival of the party's first guest. As I watched her approach, I slowly began to admit to myself that I wanted nothing more at that moment than to untie that knot on her shoulder.

That was probably the exact moment when my comprehension of "leggy" occurred, but it was also the exact moment the couple who had come in the front door behind me picked to emerge onto the deck. This set off a series of greetings and a ritualistic rubbing of cheeks as the guests met the woman coming up the stairs from the yard, but the woman hardly missed a step as she flowed right through the experience on her way to the bar.

"The color leaked out of this," she said softly, setting her glass in front of the bartender. "Could you hit it again?"

"Certainly," the bartender said, and he did it with an efficient flourish.

"Thank you," the woman said as she took a tentative sip from the glass. "From the bottom of my heart."

"You're welcome," the bartender said.

I watched this exchange without saying a word, but the woman turned in my direction and eyed me carefully over the lip of her glass. She didn't say anything while she looked, and I finally spoke when the silence had piled up as high as I could stand.

"Mrs. Gottesman?" I asked.

"Yes," she said softly. She took another sip from her glass.

"May I speak with you for a moment?"

"Isn't that what you're doing?"

"This is a private matter," I said.

"Oh, don't worry about Rafael," she said. "He's the soul of discretion. Aren't you, Rafael?"

"Absolutely," the bartender said.

"This is about Ronnie," I said.

I was expecting an answer like *Ronnie who?* but I didn't get it.

"Really?" she said, and if she missed a single beat I didn't catch it. "What about him?"

"He seems to be missing."

"And you thought I might have him stashed around here somewhere?"

"No," I said. "But I was hoping you could give me an idea about where to look."

"It has been a while since I've been able to find him myself," she said as she sipped from her glass again. "What makes *you* think he's missing?"

"He didn't show up for his gig this morning."

"Really?" she said. I watched a frown form across her forehead as she continued. "That doesn't sound like Ronnie at all."

"Exactly," I said.

"Nobody's heard from him?"

"Just Danny."

"Danny?"

I answered with a quiet nod.

"I wouldn't trust Danny any farther than I can blow him," she said. "Please excuse my French."

"Why not?" I asked.

"How well do you know him?"

"We go back quite a while."

"He's not the same guy he used to be," she said carefully. "Let's just say he has problems he can't really solve."

"You mean the gambling?" I asked.

"And the sex," she said. "Although I shouldn't talk, should I?"

I didn't know the answer to that question, so I didn't try to answer it. I just stood there and watched her take another sip from her glass.

"What's Danny's story?" she asked finally.

"Ronnie told him last night about some kind of a family emergency that he had to take care of."

"Why would he tell Danny and not Genevieve?"

"Maybe he thought Danny would make the call to Gee."

"Why would he think that? This doesn't sound like Ronnie."

"That's why I'm here," I said.

"I don't think I can help you. I haven't seen him for quite a while."

"Do you know where he's from? I'd like to check out this family emergency, but no one seems to know where to look."

"His family lives in Monroe. I know that much."

"Louisiana?"

"Were you thinking Monroe, Oregon?"

"Right," I said while I briefly envisioned a farm town smack in white Oregon's midsection producing a black disciple of Cotton Belt blues. "He could have been from there, but I guess it would have made the news."

"Well, grab a drink and circulate," she replied. "I'm glad you could make it." She said this immediately after the bartender cleared his throat slightly, and right before short, square Jack walked his horn-rimmed glasses out of the house and onto the deck.

"Oh, honey, there you are!" she said as she turned toward the house and her husband. They came together, linked arms, and began a slow descent of the stairs. I looked at the bartender, and he looked back at me.

"Do you know how to contact Gee?" I asked.

"Yes," he said simply.

"If Mrs. Gottesman hears anything or thinks of anything else, would you let us know?"

"Certainly," he said.

I turned and looked out over the yard one more time. The Gottesmans had made their way to a buffet table set up directly below me on the edge of the grass. Mrs. Gottesman unhooked her arm from her husband's and accepted a plate from a dark, wide woman decked out in a domestic uniform and an apron.

"Thank you, Maria," I heard her say. "It looks fabulous, as usual." Then her husband was served, and they both turned away from the table and began a slow reconnoiter of the yard.

"Don't think too harshly of her," the bartender said from my right. "She's really quite a wonderful person."

"Rafael, my man," I said as I watched Mrs. Gottesman's legs play mischievously with the slit in the material flowing down from the knot on her fine, slim shoulder, " 'harsh' is not the word that describes what I was thinking."

Then I moved back into the house, heading due north this time, until I eventually slipped out the front door and re-gained Alameda. From there, it was only a matter of putting one foot in front of the other again until the drifting sounds of the Gottesmans' Fourth of July party no longer hummed in my ears.

EIGHTEEN

By the time Danny climbed back into his Caddy, he had traded Larry three bills for two. *Not too bad,* he thought, *except mine were hundreds and his were a twenty and a ten. I don't know why I drive all the way out here—Leon's the only guy pulling any real money out of this damned place.*

He pointed the Caddy back at Portland, which redirected his internal dialogue to something else he didn't know—why *he* was behind the wheel instead of James. After fifteen minutes of fruitless contemplation, he cranked up his cell phone.

"What?" Lester said curtly after the third ring, although Danny could barely hear it over the boom of the blues pouring into the phone.

"We need to talk," Danny said.

"So talk."

"Move away from the damned stage! I can barely hear you."

"You wanna talk, talk. Let me worry about hearin'."

"Look, we have to do something about James."

"I heard *that.*"

"No," Danny said. "This isn't about your stupid homophobia. This is about that faggot taking a hike."

"Sounds good to me."

"Really? If he starts talking to the right people about the wrong things, how is that going to sound to you?"

"Fuckin' faggot don't have the balls."

"It doesn't take balls to talk, Lester. If you catch a little heat, it takes balls to keep your mouth shut."

"Why would he catch any heat? The cops ain't gonna pick up on this shit, believe me. People come and go in this fuckin' world all the time."

"It's not the cops I'm worried about."

"Then there ain't nothin' left to worry about," Lester said. "Those other fools'll be chasin' their own tails by the end of the day."

"Just remember what I told you," Danny said as the Caddy climbed onto the interstate bridge. "If this gets back to me, we'll be twice as screwed as we are now."

"I've got some fools comin' in from Seattle to do it, okay? It ain't gettin' back to us."

"To do what?"

"The less you know about it, the better. Remember?"

"I remember everything, Lester. It's not my memory we have to worry about."

"Good. Then we have nothin' to worry about. Can I go back to work now?"

"You better be right about James, too."

"When was the last time I was wrong about anything?"

"Geez, I don't know, Lester. But let me ask you this— when was the last time anyone ever kicked Leon's butt?"

Danny drove across the bridge and into Oregon while he waited for an answer, but all he could hear over the phone was Koko Taylor and her kickbutt Chicago blues.

"That's what I thought," Danny said finally. Then he cut the connection and tossed the phone onto the empty passenger seat.

What a piece of work this day is going to be, he said to himself. *I do believe I'm going to need a little comfort and consideration just to make it all the way to the other end.*

He let that thought curl around his brain until he could feel it all the way down to his testicles. *Or maybe it was the other way around,* he thought with a grin. He slipped off Interstate 5 and parked in the lot behind his favorite jack shack a moment later.

"Well, look who's here," Cherry said when he walked in the door.

"Happy Fourth of July," Danny said. "Do you have any fireworks here?"

"You got to bring your own fireworks, Danny. All I can do is set 'em off."

"It sounds like I came to the right place."

"You did if you came with the price of admission."

"Cherry, baby! You won't do it for love?"

"Dannyboy," Cherry said, holding her right hand out toward him and wiggling her fingers slightly. "What's love got to do with it?"

"Love is all there is, Cherry. You've been listening to the wrong song."

"Love and forty bucks for the boss, Danny, and we can go on the other side of that door and talk about the fireworks show."

"Cherry, there are girls out there who would pay *me* to see the fireworks show."

"Why aren't you talkin' to one of them, Dannyboy?"

"Do you want to know the gospel truth?" Danny asked as he peeled forty bucks off what was left of the roll in his pocket. "Love takes too damned long. Sometimes it's worth forty bucks to just sit back and let a pro do all the work."

"It's forty bucks to get behind the door, Danny. Then we'll talk about what it takes to get the pro to do all the work."

"Whatever," Danny said. "Better you than those damned vultures at Leon's."

"I couldn't agree with you more," Cherry said, sliding one arm around his waist. "I am *way* better than that."

NINETEEN

I didn't stop walking until I reached the computer located in what had once been the dining room of my house. I didn't need a dining room in those days for the same reason I didn't need a kitchen—I had no interest in food and kept none on the premises—but I inhaled information from the Internet like I needed it to breathe.

It only took a minute or two to locate a phone number for Ronnie's family in Monroe, but it took more than an hour to find out which one it was on a list of more than a hundred. It might have been an easier job if Ronnie's last name had been something other than Jones, but I didn't really mind the task of wading through the numbers. I was good at that kind of work; it reminded me of sitting at a poker table until the right cards were dealt.

When I finally dialed the right digits, I was rewarded with a voice in my ear that might have dripped out of a honey jar. "Yes?" the voice said, and it took its own sweet time to say it.

"May I speak to Ronnie, please?" I said, which was the fastest way I had found in the previous hour for getting from one number on my list to the next.

"Why, sho' you can," the voice said. "You just hang on there a second." This answer sat me up straight in my chair, but I started to sag again just as soon as the next voice came on the line.

"This is Ronnie."

"Shoot," I said. "Sounds like I've got the wrong Ronnie Jones, sir."

"I get that a lot," the Ronnie I did have said. "Or I did back when my grandson was still livin' here."

"Would your grandson be a bass-playin' fool up in Portland, Oregon, these days?"

"One and the verah same," the senior Ronnie said, but I could hear the easy grin draining out of his voice while he said it. "It do make an ol' man wonder, though."

"Sir?"

"If you know that, why you callin' Monroe?"

"Ronnie missed his gig this mornin', sir. What I'm tryin' to do here is track him down."

"Would you say that one mo' time, son?"

"Ronnie missed his gig this mornin'."

"Ronnie don't do that."

"I know. That's why we're a little spooked up here."

"What made you think he might be here?"

"We were told he had some kind of a family emergency back home."

"Ronnie tol' you that?"

"No, sir. We haven't heard from Ronnie."

"Young man, what's yo' name?"

"I'm sorry, sir. Wiley's my name."

"Wiley, don' trust whoever tol' you that no further'n you can kick 'im with yo' lef' foot. We the only fam'ly that boy's got, an' I kin tell you straight up he ain't on his way down here."

"That's exactly what I needed to know, sir."

"Now tell me what *I* need to know, son."

"Sir?"

"Gimme a number I kin reach you at when me an' the boy's grandmama git there."

"It might not be that serious, Mr. Jones."

"Ronnie missed his gig this mornin', and you didn't hear a thing from him?"

"Yes, sir."

"Let me have the number, son. We gonna be in the next two seats headed north."

TWENTY

The buzz Danny got behind Cherry's door faded before he dropped back on the freeway, and he was firmly lodged in a deficit position by the time he had the Caddy wheeling south on Front.

"Goddamned faggot!" he shouted out loud as soon as he realized he had to park the car before he could climb out of it this time.

He turned west before he reached the festival and started hunting for a parking spot. He was eight blocks from the waterfront by the time he found one, and he strode all the way back to the river in a dense swarm of self-generated expletives that only he could hear.

The festival crowd had thickened during his absence, and fans were still flowing steadily through the gates. "Fucking fireworks fans," he mumbled under his breath. "The music fans got here a long time ago."

The same cute redhead he had seen earlier beamed another smile at him as he plowed by, but his funk had folded in on him by then. *Fucking cunt,* he thought, plucking the words easily from the cloud of silent curses swirling around him.

He followed the concrete until he was standing on the lip of the bowl. Down a little and to his right, he saw Leon lounging with Ronetta. Down to Danny's left, Lester was standing in a knot of stagehands near the corner of the north stage. They were watching a zydeco band strut its stuff for a mob of people dancing deliriously in the space in front of the bandstand.

After a moment or two, Lester looked up the hill. As soon as they made eye contact, he peeled away from his buddies and began a slow stroll in Danny's direction while Danny drifted down.

"What the fuck's up your butt?" Lester asked when they met in the middle.

"I thought this was a fucking blues festival," Danny said through the music. "What's this swamp shit doing here?"

"What's with all the fuckin' cursing all of a sudden? I don't think your mama would approve."

Good question, Danny thought. *What* is *with all this cursing all of a sudden?* "She doesn't approve of you, either," Danny said. "She needs to learn to live with these small disappointments."

"Plus I remember right, you *love* this swamp shit."

"I love anything people pay money to hear, Lester. But right now I feel like stuffing that accordion down that fucking fool's throat."

"Would you fuckin' chill? How a pussy like you ever had the balls to punch that kid's ticket in the first place is beyond me."

"I didn't have to think about that. I just did it."

"Don't think about this, either."

"That's a little easier said than done."

"Fuck it is. It was just as easily done."

"What's that supposed to mean?"

"Your diversion just came down. I got the call about five minutes ago."

"Really?" Danny said, throwing a nod in Leon's general direction. "He doesn't look all that diverted."

"Stupid motherfucker don't know it yet. You watch him

a while longer, you'll see him holler just like the nursery rhyme."

"What are you talking about?"

"Eenie, meenie, minie, mo," Lester said. "We're about to catch that fuckin' nigger by the toe."

"That's very cute, Lester," Danny said softly, although he wasn't sure Lester could hear him over the two-beat heat blasting off the stage. *But if he hollers,* he wondered to himself, *who the fuck is going to make him pay the fifty fucking dollars every day?*

TWENTY-ONE

I was sitting on the floor of my front porch with my bare feet dangling down a couple of steps when Alix turned her Tercel into my driveway. She parked behind my Subaru, disembarked, strolled around the car, and climbed the stairs.

I watched her avidly as she approached, but it wasn't long before she got too close for my eyes to focus. That was when she put her mouth against mine and gave me another way to keep track of her for a moment.

"Hey," she said softly after she broke off the kiss.

"You taste like teriyaki," I said.

"Personal hygiene is always the first casualty of sitting at the festival all day."

"I wasn't complaining. I love teriyaki."

"Even so, I need to use your bathroom before you find out what else I taste like."

"I already know what else you taste like. I love that even more than teriyaki."

"I know you do," she said. She straightened up, pecked me modestly on the nose, walked by my perch on the edge of the porch, and paused at the front door. "But I have more than one flavor—and some of them are tastier than others. Give me five minutes?"

"Fine," I said. "I guess you can't do too much damage in five minutes."

"Sure I can," she said, "but I promise I won't." Then I heard her kick off her sandals and pad across Leon's handsome hardwood floor until her soft footsteps became too quiet to hear.

I spent the five minutes watching two jays flash in and out of the yard in front of the house, their blue meanderings apparently unconnected but one never far from the other. Those jays spent a lot of time around that house, and I kept an eye on them whenever our visits overlapped, because they seemed to know how to live my life better than I did.

Don't laugh—blue jays could mentor a lot of us on the subject of life. They tell the flock to fuck off, just like some of us do, but they're never alone after they do it because they mate for life. They don't pay rent, take shit, cover their colors, or kill each other, most of which I had yet to master.

Alix was still in the shower when I got there with a towel fresher than the one I had left hanging on the rack. I handed it to her as soon as she stepped out of the tub.

"Thanks," she said before she buried her face in it. I watched her move the towel around for a while, and then I watched her hang it next to mine. After that, there was nothing to watch but her.

"What'd you do with Quincy?" I asked.

"He's staying over with JJ and Scooter tonight," she said.

"You know you're missing the fireworks."

"Not true," she said. She walked past me slowly, reaching for my hand as she moved. I gave it to her, and then I let her lead me to my bedroom. When we got there, she grabbed the corner of the spread with her free hand and flipped it onto the floor. Then she did the same with the blanket and the top sheet.

"You're leaving me with no place to hide," I said as I surveyed the bedding heaped on the floor.

"Also not true," she said, climbing onto the naked sheet and stretching out on her back. "You need to look a little closer."

I straddled her on the bed with one knee on each side of her thin waist, the curve of her hips warm against the bare legs sticking out of my gym shorts. I leaned forward, dropped my hands on the bed, and propped myself over her while I kissed her forehead softly.

She ran both hands under my T-shirt until she had each of my nipples surrounded by a thumb and a finger. "Take your shirt off, Wiley," she said as she squeezed.

I straightened up, slipped the shirt over my head, and dropped it on top of the bedding on the floor. "Bring these down here," she said when I was done, tugging on my nipples as she said it.

I leaned forward again, this time lining up first her right hand and then her left with her mouth. She replaced her thumbs and her fingers with her tongue and her teeth when I did this, but for some reason I could feel the resulting sensations even more intensely somewhere else than I could at the points of application.

"I love your nipples, Wiley," she said after a moment or two.

"Sure, you say that now while I'm young and studly. When I'm old and fat, what then?"

"Then you'll have some cute little breasts to go with the nips. That'll be even better."

"I can't wait," I said, and then I kissed her. It was soft and tender when it started, but it was long; by the time I came up for air, the kiss had turned hard and so had I. I knew the erection wouldn't last, but I enjoyed the feel of it while I started moving my kisses around on Alix's breathtaking body.

I took my time while I did it. You hear people say "It's not the destination, it's the journey" all the time, but I don't believe it could ever be more true than it is when making love to a beautiful woman. I started with the scar just below her breast—a souvenir from a very bad man with a very sharp knife—even though the memory unearthed by running my tongue along that seam made both of us shudder. I liked starting there; it reminded me of how far we had come, how fortunate we had been, and how much we had lost along the way.

After the scar, Alix's shudders were for all the right reasons. I drew as many out of her as she could stand; almost as soon as she absolutely insisted, I moved up to nestle beside her.

"God, I needed that," she said.

"Me, too. I think it all started with that blonde in the blue tank top."

"It started a long time before that."

"Yeah. I guess it did."

"You know what I like about you, Wiley?"

"What?"

"The fact that I love you."

"You *like* me because you *love* me?"

"I'm serious," she said softly. "It feels different knowing that I love you. I like it."

"We did this before you loved me," I said.

"I know," she said, and she locked her Asian eyes on me while she said it. "I did a lot of things with a lot of people before I loved you. That's why I know the difference."

"I don't love *you* like that, Alix."

"I know," she said. "But that's your problem, not mine." Then she kissed me softly on the lips and crinkled her nose at me.

"What?" I asked.

"You're right," she said. "I *do* taste better than teriyaki."

"I rest my case."

"I think not. First I get to find out what *you* taste like."

"I guess a girl's gotta do what a girl's gotta do," I said magnanimously, but the phone rang before she got a chance to get started.

"Can we just let it ring?" she asked, running both hands up my legs until they disappeared under my gym shorts.

"Talked me into it," I said, but a moment later my machine kicked in and turned her hands to ice.

"Uh, this is Richard Jameson," a man said faintly from the dining room, the voice identifiable but dehydrated somehow since I had first heard it come out of the professor's mouth that morning. I reached over Alix to pick up the receiver on the nightstand next to the bed.

"I'm here," I said.

"Thank God," he said, and then he didn't speak again for a moment. I waited for the moment to end, but as soon as it did I wanted it back again.

"I'm afraid we need you out here right away," he said finally.

"We?" I asked.

"Well, I guess *I* need you, actually. Julie didn't want me to call."

"Professor," I said, an icy fist slowly forcing my intestines into unnatural configurations as I said it, "what the fuck are you talking about?"

"It's Julie," he said, and I don't know what he said after that because I vaulted over Alix and hit the floor running.

TWENTY-TWO

Danny slid deep inside Sara Sue, and it was as easy as it was sweet because she was slicker than hot oil by the time he started.

This right here is what it's all about, Danny thought. *Foreplay is* way *overrated.* "Is this what you wanted?" he asked.

"It might be," she said. "Ask me fifteen or twenty minutes from now."

"You'll be wrung out and hung up to dry a long time before that."

"Show me, Danny, don't fuckin' tell me about it."

Danny had a sudden urge to slap Sara Sue in the mouth, but the fact that he had her bent over the edge of the bed with her face buried in the sheets made that hard to accomplish. He channeled the urge through his hips instead and proceeded to pound her mercilessly, but she settled in around him and rocked right back.

"Yessss!" she cried a few minutes later, but Danny steamed straight through that one and three or four more just like it before he finally finished. He dropped on the bed beside her, and she snuggled in close.

"God, I needed that," she said.

"Mister Muscles isn't getting it done?"

"Fuckin' steroids," she said. "That shit ruined a perfectly fine man, Danny."

"My heart goes out to the both of you."

"Maybe if you *had* a heart it would."

"Well, yes, if I did."

"That's okay, Dannyboy. It wasn't a heart that I needed tonight."

"I'm happy to lend a helping hand."

"It wasn't a hand, either. Really, I don't know how you keep that thing goin' as long as you do. You're quite the phenomenon, Danny."

"I could say the same about you, baby."

"Go ahead."

"You were the best fuck of the day, by far."

"I'm not sure how much of a compliment that is, Danny. Maybe this was a slow day for you."

"A gentleman doesn't keep a running count, Sara Sue."

"I'll bet you do, though."

"Three," Danny said through a grin. "So far."

"Really?" Sara Sue said, rolling up on top of him so she could stare straight into his eyes. "You are one sick motherfucker, aren't you?"

"Perhaps. But I think you have the same disease."

"That's right," she said, turning so her face was pointing toward his feet and everything in between. "And as soon as I get this thing of yours back up, Dannyboy, we're gonna see if we can run your count any higher than three."

TWENTY-THREE

Forest Grove is usually forty-five minutes by car from north-east Portland, but Alix's Tercel didn't take that long. Neither of us said a word on the way; Alix lost herself in the simple mechanics of freeway driving, while I sat dumbly in the seat next to her and let memories of my former life bury me alive.

We went back a long way in that town, Julie and I, which is why I normally never went near the place. I had come to the university to play some point guard and pick up a teaching degree, Julie and the daughter we had made during a moment of madness in high school dragging along behind me like an afterthought. More than two decades later, I was living alone in Portland and our daughter wasn't living any-where; but Julie was still there, in the house formerly known as ours, and I was riding in her direction with nothing *but* af-terthoughts on my mind.

Jameson met us at the front door when we got there, but the look in the round eyes behind his glasses said he wasn't too sure exactly where he was.

"What happened, Professor?" I asked.

"I'm not a professor, actually," he said vaguely as he ush-ered us inside. "I'm not that high on the food chain around here."

"Just tell me what happened," I said flatly.

"I'm sorry," he said, blinking his eyes as if it might help him focus somehow. "Of course." Then his voice trailed off as though the vocabulary of a university nonprofessor were inadequate to the task in front of him.

"Where's Julie?" I asked when it looked like his voice was unlikely to break through on its own.

"She's upstairs," he said. "But she doesn't want to see you—she's quite adamant about that. She's furious with me for calling you after she told me not to."

"Spit it out, Jameson. I'm here, and neither of you can do anything about it now."

"She was raped, Wiley. Twice. Right in front of me, and I couldn't do a damned thing about that, either."

"I'm going up," Alix said, and I watched her take the stairs leading from the living room to the bedrooms above two at a time.

"What happened?" I asked Jameson again after Alix had climbed out of my sight.

"There were two men with guns waiting for us when we got here," he said, his voice finally flowing but oddly off pitch. "They jumped us on the front porch, forced us inside, and then took turns raping her. Right here. Right in front of me."

"How badly is she hurt?"

"They didn't have to hurt her to do it—not physically, anyway. They just pressed a gun to the side of my head and threatened to pull the trigger if she didn't do whatever they said."

I had nothing handy to say to that, so nothing is what I said. Jameson matched me word for silent word for a while, but he finally found his voice again. "You can't imagine how utterly useless that made me feel," he said, staring at the carpet in front of his feet.

He couldn't have been more wrong, but I didn't take the time to correct him. *You should have seen me standing next to our daughter's slab at the morgue,* I thought. *I know all about useless.*

"You probably saved her life," I said. "She would have fought them if you hadn't been here."

"That's a very generous way to look at it," he said.

"We're *all* lucky you were with her, Jameson. She would have forced them to use those guns."

"I suppose," he said, looking up at me before he wandered a couple of steps to his right and sprawled on the couch that Julie had found at a garage sale a lifetime ago.

"Did you call the cops?" I asked.

"No."

"Why not?"

"They said they'd come back and kill everyone in the house if we did."

"What happened when they were done?"

"When they were done?" he asked blankly, as if I had suddenly switched to a language in which he did not have a graduate degree.

"I assume they aren't still here," I said.

"Oh," he said. "They left. When they were done."

"In what?"

"I don't know. They walked out that door right there, and I haven't seen them since."

"Did you see a car outside when you got here?"

"No. There was nothing in the driveway or out in front."

"Where'd they come from when they jumped you?"

"It was like they popped out of the rhododendron by the steps. I guess they came from the Cedar Street side of the house."

"Did you see a car parked over there when you drove up?"

"Maybe. There might have been something there."

"Have you ever seen either of the men before?"

"Never. Of that, I'm certain."

"What'd they look like?"

"I don't know. It sounds stupid, but I didn't really look at them."

"Big or small?"

"One big, one very big."

"Dark or light?"

"White guys, I guess. A couple of racist white guys."

"What?" I said, like *I* was suddenly the one who didn't know the language.

"The bigger one said something like 'Too bad it's not the nigger bitch.' Then the other one said, 'I still don't get why you wanna fuck a nigger. This one's fine with me.'"

"When did this come up?"

"Right before they—you know, at the beginning."

I started to notice at that point in the conversation that the ice in my gut was drawing all the heat out of my body. I could feel my temperature falling while I stood there trying to process Jameson's comments, and after a while I couldn't stand there any longer.

"Can you wait here for me? I'll be back down in a minute."

"She doesn't want to see you," he said, glancing at the stairs. "She made that abundantly clear, believe me."

"Don't worry about it," I said. "She already knows that I don't really *care* what she wants."

I inhaled the stairs in three or four gulps and turned left when I got to the top. Julie was stretched out on what had once been our bed with a washcloth pressed to her face, and Alix was doing the pressing from her perch on the edge of the bed.

"I don't want you here, Wiley," Julie said when she saw me. "I told Richard not to call you."

"He did the right thing," I said.

"No. He did not. The *last* thing I want is you and Leon pulling another stupid macho thing because of this."

"What we do isn't really up to you, Julie."

"You can say that again."

"Look, there are some things you have to do."

"Don't look now, Wiley, but what *I* do isn't really up to you."

"You need to see a doctor. You need to talk to the police."

"I have no intention of doing either one."

"It's standard operating procedure, Julie."

"What the fuck difference does it make to you? You're not even an extra in this production anymore, remember?"

"I'd like to make sure you're okay."

"I've been fucked before, Wiley," she said. Then she rose slowly from the bed, placing her hand briefly on Alix's shoulder as she walked by. "A hot shower, and I'll be fine."

I blocked the doorway into the upstairs hall with my arm. "A shower changes everything," I said.

"How lucky for me," she said. "Let me by, please."

I dropped my arm to my side, and she slid around me and into the hall. "Is Richard still here?" she asked when she reached the bathroom doorway.

"Yes."

"Do one thing for me, would you?"

"Yes," I said.

"Ask him to leave. I don't think I can deal with him right now." Then she walked into the bathroom and closed the door behind her.

I turned back toward the bed and Alix. She was sitting there looking at me quietly, and she shook her head when she saw me begin to speak. "Until you've been there," she said softly, "you have no fuckin' idea."

"Is there anything I can do?" I asked.

"Just do what she asked you to do," she said. "Tell the fuckin' professor to go home."

TWENTY-FOUR

"This is going to be the end of us, isn't it?" Jameson asked.

"I have no idea," I said.

"How could it not be?"

I didn't know the answer to that question, so I didn't offer one. He looked at me hopefully for a moment; then the hope evaporated, and he walked around me to the door.

"Tell her I'll call," he said, and I promised I would as I closed the door behind him. I listened to his footsteps on the porch, the slam of his car door, and the cough of the engine cranking up, but I listened from a great distance. My mind clamped down on what he had been able to tell me, but the information refused to line up in a row no matter how hard I hammered at it.

I drifted into the dining room and punched enough numbers into the phone to hook up with Leon's cell. "Talk to me," he said into my ear, his voice barely audible under the thunder of the fireworks show at the festival.

I honored his request, and when I was finished I shut my mouth and listened to the boom of recreational explosives while Leon's mind went to work on the same muddle that had stymied mine.

"What the fuck," he said finally.

"Yeah," I replied. "These aren't some random rapists, are they?"

"No," he said, his voice still almost too quiet to hear through the background clamor. "So who the fuck are they?"

"Question number one," I said.

"And why?"

"Question number two."

"Try to get Julie out of there while we're workin' on the answers."

"That would be good," I said slowly.

"But?"

"She probably won't go."

"Yeah," Leon said, and then I didn't hear anything but fireworks for a while. By the time Leon's voice returned, I could hear a new edge in it.

"Let's do it *that* way, then. I'll bring everyone out there."

"These motherfuckers know about this place, Leon."

"Until we find out what the fuck is goin' on," he said, "we're gonna have to circle the wagons no matter where we go. I'll bring a little help."

"She won't like that, either."

"She don't have to like it, bro'. Gimme sixty minutes, max."

"You got it," I said, and then the fireworks faded to nothing in my ear and he was gone. I hung up Julie's phone and walked back into the living room.

Where did it happen? I wondered. *Right there on the couch? On the floor, maybe?* I tried to visualize the scene from the scraps I had gleaned from Jameson, but I failed. Either I didn't have enough pieces to put the puzzle together or I didn't really want to assemble the pieces I had, but either way I was still standing there in a quiet daze several minutes later when Alix came down the stairs.

"How is she?" I asked.

"It'll be a long time before anyone knows the answer to that question," she said.

"Should I go up?"

"She's asleep."

"That might be the best thing, all things considered."

"Don't believe everything she says."

"Julie doesn't lie at all, Alix."

"I said that wrong. Just don't start thinking that whatever she says is *all* she is feeling at the time. Believe me, this kind of thing kicks up a lot of shit."

"I do," I said, and I stepped close and wrapped my arms around her.

"You do what?"

"Believe you. She's lucky you're here."

"She's lucky *you're* here, too. And she probably knows it."

"Well, we'll all be here soon."

"You talked to Leon, then?"

"They're on the way."

"Good," she said quietly, her cheek pressed close to mine.

"You're sure?"

"Absolutely," she said, and she did the same thing with her arms that I was doing with mine as she said it. "I don't know what's goin' on, Wiley, but I do know where I want to be while we find out."

TWENTY-FIVE

I don't know how long my internal sonar system had been on tilt, but the sound of sidewalk fireworks suddenly penetrated my consciousness when I came out of my clinch with Alix.

"Let's go across the street for a minute," I said.

"Why?"

"The bomb squad over there might have seen something earlier."

"You go," she said. "I want to be here if Julie needs anything." She kissed me softly on the lips, and I kissed her back the same way. Then she headed for the stairs, and I went out the front door. I turned left at the rhododendron, walked under its branches, and popped out on the sidewalk along Cedar Street.

The night sky was clear, but the acrid residue of phosphorus clung to the hazy air near the ground like the breath of two or three fire-breathing dragons. I watched the jumble of kids waving sparklers and lighting firecrackers across the street for a moment, and when the moment was over I sent my feet where my eyes were pointed.

"Long time no see," the biggest of the kids said when I got to him.

"I know," I said. "I swear you're twice as tall as the last time I saw you."

"It hasn't been *that* long," he said with a smile. "But I'm workin' on it."

"You been here all day?" I asked.

"Pretty much."

"You see a couple of guys sitting across the street in a car earlier?"

"Yeah. They were there a while."

"Big white guys?"

"Big and real big."

"What kind of car?"

"Barracuda," he said. "A '66, I think, or a '67. Could have been a nice one, but they hadn't done that much with it."

"You remember anything else?"

"Kind of rust-colored, dual pipes, decent set of speakers," he said with a shrug as he fired off a string of miniature explosions. "It was nothin' special."

"You see the guys get out of the car?"

"Yeah. They went in the house after Julie got home."

"Can you tell me anything about them?"

"You don't know 'em?" he said, looking up from the fireworks he was fumbling with on the sidewalk.

"Not yet," I said.

"I didn't really pay that much attention to 'em, Wiley. The short one was built pretty good. The tall one was really fat. They both had brown hair and real short crew cuts. That's about all I remember."

"What were they wearing?"

"I dunno. Shorts and T-shirts, I guess. No—they both had those shirts with flowers all over 'em."

"Long shirts. The kind that hang loose."

"Yeah. The ones that button down the front."

"How long were they in the house?"

"I don't know for sure. The hot dogs got done about then, so we moved to the backyard for a while."

"When you came back out, the car was gone."

"Yeah."

"Look, Araby," I said. I'm not sure why I started like that, because the kid had been looking up at me unblinkingly for quite a while by that time. "If you ever see either of those guys again, or the car, call the house immediately."

"You still have the same number?"

"The house does."

"What's goin' on, Wiley?"

"I don't know," I said, and I turned away from his insistent gaze and gaped at the empty space across the street where an undernourished Barracuda had been parked earlier in the day. I heard Araby's little brothers squealing with delight amid a series of small explosions, but I think I was only registering every third or fourth round. A silence that was not really there somehow engulfed me periodically, and I stood and let it do whatever it wanted with me.

"I just thought of something else," Araby said finally. He got up and moved next to me, his head easily even with my shoulder, his eyes pointed in the same direction as mine. "The 'Cuda had Washington plates."

"Thanks," I said. "That's good to know. You think of anything else, be sure to call. Okay?"

"Okay."

"Your mom and dad out back?"

"Right next to the cooler," he said. "They didn't see anything, Wiley."

"Independence Day will come for real one of these years, Araby."

"I guess it did for you, huh?"

"More or less."

"More or less? What the heck does that mean, anyway?"

"I'm free, but I'm still here right now. Maybe that's what it means."

"I'd settle for that."

"You're not alone there, kid," I said, and I wrapped my arm around him and squeezed. *Sure as shit,* I thought as I turned him loose and started back across the street, *you are not alone there.*

TWENTY-SIX

Danny had no trouble finding the house; it was half a block off Sandy just like Dexter had said it was. He parked the Caddy where Dexter had said to park, and a moment later Dexter opened the door for him.

"Glad you could make it," Dexter said. "We've got one seat left, and it's just your size."

"Doesn't one size pretty much fit all?" Danny asked as Dexter ushered him into a room originally designed for a sofa, a television, and a reclining chair or two. Dexter had gone a different direction, though: The room was furnished with a circular table covered with blue felt and surrounded by eleven well-padded chairs. One of the chairs had a dealer Danny didn't know sitting in it, and one chair three seats to the dealer's right was empty.

"Hey, fellas," Danny said as he moved around to the open seat. "Now's the time to pick 'em up and leave."

"Gee," Leonard said. "Are we gonna get another lesson, Danny?"

"Am I ever glad to see you, Leonard. I really appreciate you bringing my money back to me like this."

"All the money I brought is mine."

"Same thing," Danny said with a grin. "What are you playing here, Dexter?"

"Ten-twenty," Dexter said.

"I don't have that kind of cash on me, Dex."

"Your marker's good with me, Danny, you know that. How much you want?"

"Give me a thousand, and write this down somewhere—I gave all these fools fair warning."

"Get Danny a rack, sweetheart," Dexter said, and his sweetheart got up from her stool behind a kitchen counter choked with poker chips and ambled a rack over to Danny.

"Blow on them for me, Louise," Danny said. "For luck."

"I'm not that lucky, Danny," she said as she planted the chips on the table in front of him. "You'd be better off takin' 'em like they are."

"Come on now, Louise. The only woman in here with all these red-blooded American men—what could be luckier than that?"

"That's pretty much the point I'm tryin' to make."

"Ouch!" Danny said as he looked Louise over once or twice. "You hear that, fellas?" Some of the fellas acknowledged hearing that and some didn't, and when Danny caught Louise by the eye for an instant she appeared to be lined up with the fellas who didn't.

You definitely aren't what you were a few years ago, Danny thought. *It's a good thing I got you when I did.* Then he turned his attention to the game, which eventually swallowed the rack Louise had brought him and three more just like it.

TWENTY-SEVEN

Leon was at one end of Julie's dining room table, and I was at the other. I was staring at the backs of my eyelids, my elbows planted on the table and my chin resting on my thumbs. That put my hands in front of my mouth, which might have impaired communication somewhat except that I had nothing to say.

Leon was slouched in his chair, his legs stretched out under the table and his arms crossed. His slitted eyes were first cousins to shut tight, but they had no trouble tracking what was going on in the room because no one but Junior had moved appreciably in three or four hours.

Junior was hired help, but he wasn't being paid to think, so he had abandoned the table in favor of the living room sofa. The kids had been whisked off to the back room almost immediately upon arrival, and Ronetta had vanished up the same stairs that the other two women in the house had used to disappear without a trace. That left Leon and me, spinning our wheels at opposite ends of a long table while the night outside slowly became a new day.

Eventually, I leaned back in my chair and opened my eyes. "Still nothing?" I asked.

"Nothing but questions," Leon answered.

"You still don't see this as random, then."

"Two guys with guns drive down from Washington, park alongside the house for most of the afternoon, rape Julie when she gets home, and then drive off? I don't see that as random, no."

"They didn't necessarily drive down from Washington," I said. "You move here from another state, you don't always change your plates right away."

"Either way, we know they don't live around here."

"We do?"

"If you might bump into your victim at the supermarket, you have to make an attempt to hide your identity."

"Or leave no witnesses behind."

"Exactly. So the same questions remain: Why here, why now?"

"And why in a car every kid like Araby is sure to notice?"

"That doesn't seem too smart, does it?"

"Actually," I said, "it seems a little *too* stupid."

"Maybe we're not lookin' at the picture right."

"Is there some way that makes these idiots look smarter?"

"The car leads us in the wrong direction, how smart are they?"

"How do they even know there's an us?"

"That's why these questions are kickin' my ass," he said. "Too damned many, too damned good."

"Maybe we have to start the same place no matter what the answers are."

"Maybe. You think Sam would do us a favor?"

"I guess that depends on how homicide detectives feel about the people who supply them with new cases," I said, thinking back on half a dozen deaths we had been more or less related to during the past two years.

"Haven't we been friends since high school?" Leon asked.

"Friends might be too strong a word," I said, thinking back a lot further than a couple of years to a series of basketball games in which we had made one of the best post players in the state look like a fool. "He probably hated our guts back then."

"True. But I think he hates the *real* bad guys a lot more than he hates us."

"Even if he's willing, what can he do for us? Julie won't cooperate, and this isn't Sam's jurisdiction, anyway." I didn't add that this wasn't a homicide case, either, but I was afraid he'd say "It's going to be" so I just let that slide.

"Ask him if a '66 or '67 Barracuda was reported stolen in Washington during the last day or two."

"What does that tell us?" I asked, although I might not have needed the explanation if I had slept even briefly during that night.

"If the answer is yes, they know there's an us for sure. And they're nowhere near as stupid as they look." Then his voice trailed off, and he locked his fingers behind his head and stretched his neck muscles for a moment.

"What?" I asked.

"If that's all true," he said slowly, his eyes actually closing for real as he spoke, "this thing ain't really about Julie at all."

"It's about us," I said, and I didn't need a question mark at the end of the sentence.

"Yeah," he said. "But why?"

"I can only think of one thing goin' on that's out of the ordinary."

"Same here," he said. "Which has an upside, that's for sure."

"You lost me there."

"We know where to start with that other thing," Leon said. "And God help Dannyboy if he's dirty with this shit, because he'll get no motherfuckin' mercy from me."

TWENTY-EIGHT

"Rough night," Dexter said around seven in the morning. Everyone had drifted out of the house except the three of them—the host, the hostess, and Danny.

"No kidding," Danny said.

"Sorry the game broke up while you were down," Dexter said. "I know how frustrating it can be when it goes like that."

"No kidding," Danny said again.

"Look, we can go head to head for a while if you want. I'd like to give you a chance to win your money back."

"Dexter, you just read my mind," Danny said, but he wasn't looking at Dexter when he said it. He was watching the way Louise tipped her head back when she exhaled the smoke she was drawing from the cigarette burning in her hand. *You took me almost as deep as that smoke,* he thought. *You were something, Louise, I kid you not.*

"Sweetheart," Dexter said, "would you mind dealing a few hands for us?"

Louise snubbed out the cigarette in an ashtray on the counter and stepped away from her stool. "How much do you want?" she asked.

"What do you think, Danny?" Dexter said.

"No limit?"

"That's fine."

"How about six grand? That would give me a chance to finish ahead."

"Six racks each, sweetheart," Dexter said, and Louise walked six racks to the table and went back to the counter for six more. Danny watched her coming and going, and when she returned he watched that, too.

He was still watching as Louise took the seat behind the dealer's slot and picked up a deck of cards. She was wearing a simple sleeveless blouse that buttoned down the front, and the top three or four buttons were apparently superfluous. Danny eyed her sweet cleavage as Louise shuffled the cards.

"High card starts with the button," she said, and she tossed a red queen in front of Dexter and a black ace in Danny's direction.

"I'm a winner already, Dex," Danny said. "Last chance to reconsider."

"I'm not that smart, Danny," Dexter said softly, but there was something near the bottom of his voice that turned Danny's head. *What?* Danny thought. *You don't like me looking at your sweetheart?*

Dexter looked back at him blankly, his innocent eyes behind bifocals that should have been on an accountant somewhere. He was shorter, thinner, and older than Danny, but Danny knew he wasn't dumber.

"Yeah, right," Danny said, and then he hunkered down for thirty minutes while he and Dexter traded antes aimlessly. Then Louise dealt him a pair of aces in the hole and the game began. He was back on the button then, so Dexter had to act first.

"Five hundred," Dexter said.

"Whatever," Danny said. "I'll make a donation for lack of anything better to do."

Louise flopped an ace, a king, and a deuce, and Dexter looked over at Danny for a moment. "I check," he said.

"Don't look at me," Danny said. "I can wait if you can."

Louise turned a seven, and Dexter looked at Danny some more. "What the heck," he said. "Maybe I can buy this for a grand." He pushed that much toward the middle of the table, and Danny did the same.

"Heck," Danny said. "I'll see one more card." Louise added a four to the cards on the table, and Dexter looked at the four, and then he looked at Danny.

"I think I've got you beat," he said. "I'm gonna bet it all, Danny."

"Send it over, Dex," Danny said, flashing his aces. "After all these years, your sweetheart here turns out to be my lucky dealer."

"Son of a bitch," Dexter said, but he said it so quietly Danny wasn't sure if he heard the words or just read Dexter's lips. Dexter turned over the ace and king of spades and stared at them like a more thorough examination might somehow make two pair better than three of a kind.

"You outplayed me on this one, Danny. I had you on one ace, not two."

"That was the plan, man," Danny said through a grin. Then he leaned toward Louise and dropped a pair of fifty-dollar chips into the gap in her blouse.

"And you say that you aren't lucky," he said. Louise turned her head slowly in Danny's direction and looked at him, but he could see nothing in her eyes that he could translate into his native language. After a silent second or two, she turned her blank attention to Dexter.

"You done?" she asked.

"Danny?" he said.

"Are you kidding me? I'm the only guy at this gold mine with a shovel, Dex. You'll have to chase me out of here with a stick."

"Do you mind, sweetheart?"

Louise rose from her seat, walked to the counter, and came back with another armload of chips. Then she sat down, shuffled the cards, and dealt for two more hours before the curtain finally fell.

It started with two black kings. As soon as Danny saw them, he pushed a thousand dollars into the pot. Dexter thought it over for a couple of minutes, but he finally did the same. Then Louise flopped the king and queen of diamonds with the four of hearts.

Danny recounted his kings, and as soon as he got to three he added another couple of grand to the pot. Dexter sat there like he was trying to count something, too, but it was taking him a lot longer.

"Forget those damned diamonds," Danny said. "I'm the one with the lucky dealer, Dex."

"Apparently," Dexter said softly. "But I'm not convinced this is really about luck, actually. I'll call that two grand, Danny."

"Show him what I'm talking about, Louise," Danny said, and Louise dropped the six of clubs on the table. Dexter stared at it like it had an extra cloverleaf or two, and Danny leaned back and watched him do it.

"I'm guessing that six doesn't do much for you," he said after he had seen enough.

"You got that right," Dexter said.

"I'll tell you what, Dex. You want to stare at another card, you're going to have to pay for it. I'm betting it all."

Dexter tipped his head up a notch or two and looked through his glasses at Danny. "That's more than I have on the table," he said, his voice still so quiet that Danny could see the words almost as well as he could hear them.

"Your marker is good with me, Dex, you know that."

"What do you have there? Twelve grand and change?"

"Something like that."

"I'll call that, Danny."

"You hear that, Louise? Dexter doesn't believe these kings you gave me are good enough."

"She has a lot of cards over there that will beat three kings, Danny."

"Maybe so," Danny said, his grin really running away with itself this time. "But Louise won't do that to me. Isn't that right, sweetheart?"

Louise burned the top card on the deck and turned over the two of diamonds. She looked at the card, then placed the deck on the table and looked up at Danny. "Apparently not," she said.

Danny's eyes ran from the card to Louise to Dexter, who was turning over the ten and jack of diamonds, and then they blurred for a moment or two and he couldn't see shit.

"Well," he heard Dexter say. "My flush is a winner. Imagine that!" Then he heard Louise slide her chair away from the table, and he blinked his eyes back to working order.

"What?" he asked. "You're quitting on me?"

"I wouldn't want to stretch you too thin," Dexter said as Louise strolled back to the counter. "I imagine ten grand will be enough of a challenge for you."

"Tell that cocksucking bitch this game isn't over," Danny said.

"This is as far as I'm willing to go," Dexter said.

"I don't give a fuck what you're willing to do."

Dexter blinked once behind his glasses, then directed his gaze at Louise. When Danny turned to do the same, he saw a shortened shotgun pointed at his face. "Are you trying to threaten me, Danny?" Dexter said.

"Of course not," Danny said. "Put that thing away."

"Monday morning, Danny. As soon as the banks open would be best."

Danny swiveled in his chair again. Dexter sat there looking

at him quietly, his eyes still blank, the bifocals still fixed on the wrong face.

"So that's it?"

"For now, I think that's best. Don't you?"

"Fuck you, Dex," Danny said, but he got up while he said it and started toward the door.

"Sweetheart, would you mind cashing Danny out?" Dexter said.

"What the fuck are you talking about?" Danny said. He looked toward the counter soon enough to see Louise extract the poker chips from inside her blouse.

"We owe you for these," she said.

"Fuck both of you," Danny said. Then he started moving his feet again, and this time he was on the far side of the door to his car before he stopped.

TWENTY-NINE

"Sam Adams," Sam said.

"This is Sunday morning, Sam," I said.

"People get killed on Sundays."

"Plus you still haven't found all the people who killed people yesterday."

"Yeah," he said. "Plus that. Which means I really don't have time to shoot the shit here, Wiley."

"I was going to ask for a favor, actually."

"So this won't be a confession, then."

"Aren't confessions for the guilty?"

"Exactly," Sam said. "What's the favor?"

"Can you find out if a '66 or '67 Barracuda has been reported stolen in Washington?"

"Probably. If I wanted to."

"You want to, Sam."

"For old time's sake?"

"Will that work?"

"No."

"Pick a reason that does work, Sam. You want to do it, believe me."

"Where are you?"

"I'm at Julie's, but I don't know for how long. You still have Leon's number?"

"I've had his number since day one."

"Yeah," I said. "Well, that's probably the best one to use."

He didn't respond to that, so I listened to his silence until it ended. "That's all you have to say?" he asked finally.

It took me a moment to figure out how to answer that, so when I did I continued to stand there with my mouth shut.

"Jeezus Christ," Sam muttered, and then the phone went dead in my ear. I looked over at Leon, who was still stretched out in the same chair at the same end of the same dining room table Julie's dad had made when she was a kid.

"What'd he say?" Leon asked quietly.

"Jeezus Christ," I said.

"Always was an eloquent son of a bitch," he said, and then he closed his eyes and settled down to wait.

THIRTY

Danny drove for fifteen or twenty minutes before he noticed where he was going. The Caddy was streaming east on Interstate 80, and Danny put an end to that madness when he saw Troutdale flash by on his right. He pulled off the freeway at the state park exit and paused in the parking area for a moment.

One trip out here this week is already too many, he whispered into his inner ear. Meanwhile, his inner eye watched a replay of Ronnie's last ride in the same direction two nights earlier. Then he shook that image off and reached for his phone.

How about Serena? he thought. *I could use some serenity right now.* He scrolled through his numbers until he found the right one, and five rings later Serena was on the line.

"No shit?" she said when he identified himself. "This must be my lucky day."

"Absolutely," Danny said. "I can be at your place in five minutes, max."

"You do that, Danny, and I'm gonna like it a lot more than you will."

"Don't tell me you're still hot about that."

"Oh, no. I'm cold as hell about it now."

"Don't try to tell me you didn't love it, sweetheart. The booty doesn't lie, believe me."

"Here's something *you* can believe, Danny. The next time I see your face, I'm gonna smash it in with a baseball bat. Did you say that's gonna be about five minutes from now?"

"To tell you the truth, Serena, that's not the kind of action I'm looking for."

"This isn't my lucky day, then?"

"I guess not."

"Then get off my fuckin' phone," she said before she slammed her receiver in Danny's ear.

"Stupid bitch," Danny said out loud, thinking back to the romp with Serena that had taken a sour turn as soon as Danny changed channels without her consent. "Who is she trying to kid? I know for a fact she liked every minute of it."

He climbed out of the car and walked until only Jesus could have walked any farther. The river seemed bluer than usual under the hard glint of the morning sun, and Danny stood there quietly and stared at it until his eyes couldn't take the shimmering glare any longer.

He looked down at the phone in his hand, located another number, and started a new conversation. "Guess where I am," he said.

"Who is this?"

"Who were you just dreaming would call?"

"Are you crazy?"

"Somewhat," Danny said. "But you love me like that."

"What if Phil had picked up the phone? Don't you understand how dangerous it is to call me here?"

"I'd say screw Phil, except he's not the one I really want."

"I'm serious, Danny!"

"So am I, sweetheart."

"You're lucky, you know that? You're *really* lucky. Any other Sunday morning, you'd be talkin' to him right now."

"I'm not that crazy. I'd have hung up by now, believe me."

"Great. He kicks my ass every time he gets a hangup, just in case it had something to do with me."

"Why do you stay with that stupid prick?"

"That's none of your business, Danny."

"True. Let's talk about what *is* my business. Guess where I am."

"He's back. Please—*don't* call me here again." Then she severed the connection, and Danny was left with the sparkling Sandy River in front of him and the echo of another voice in his ear.

"What the hell is going on?" he said. "Now I can't even get a jump when I need one?"

The Sandy absorbed his question, but he couldn't decipher what the river whispered in reply.

"Just shut the fuck up," he said after he had heard more of the blue murmurs than he could handle. "What did I ever do to deserve all this shit?"

THIRTY-ONE

"Do I know him?" Julie asked. She was looking out her bedroom window at Junior, who had his bald head and all his muscles surrounded by his car across the street.

"No," I said.

"I *really* hate all this," she said.

"I know."

"I don't think you do. I don't think you have a fucking clue."

"Can you explain it to me?"

"I don't owe you an explanation, Wiley. You owe me."

I made no reply to that because no reasonable reply came to mind. What I did instead was continue to lean against her doorjamb while she struggled with the modification of her view that Leon and I had made.

"The kids are cooking downstairs," I said after a couple of uneasy minutes of silence. "Do you want something to eat?"

"No," she said flatly as she turned in my direction. "I want you guys out of my house."

"We need to find out what's goin' on before we leave you guys alone out here."

"This is almost like being raped all over again," she said. "Don't you see that?"

"Yes."

"Then why are you doing it?"

"Rape isn't the worst thing that can happen to you, Julie. Or to the kids."

"What are you talking about? This happens to someone every fucking day. You don't have to make this big drama out of it."

"It might not be that simple."

"This is all part of something else?"

"It might be."

"Jesus," she said. She shook her head slowly and turned back to the window. I stood dumbly in her bedroom doorway and admired the elegant curve of her neck until she bounced a few more words off the glass in front of her.

"How long ago did you walk out of here?" she asked.

"You know when it was," I said.

"And you can't say you were ever really with me from the beginning, can you?"

"No."

"Then why the fuck are you here now? Can you explain that to me, Wiley?"

"I doubt it," I said. "In order to do that, I'd have to understand it myself."

"Your self-awareness just overwhelms me, Wiley."

"Oh, I think you're handling it pretty well."

"Go down and eat," she said, still gazing out her window as if a hard glare might make Junior disappear. "I'd like to have *this* room to myself, at least."

I went down without another word, but I didn't eat. I hadn't been hungry for a year and a half or more, and not a single thing happened on that trip to the Grove to accelerate my appetite.

THIRTY-TWO

"What the fuck is it now?" Lester said.

"I'm not in the mood for your attitude," Danny said.

"Stick that phone up your ass instead of your ear, you won't hear it anymore."

"Motherfucking cocksucker!" Danny shouted as he hit his brakes hard to avoid ramming his Caddy up the ass of a Honda Accord.

"I *know* you're not talkin' to me," Lester said.

"Fuckin' drivers," Danny said.

"You need to chill out, man, I mean it. You take a little heat and profanity pops out all over the fuckin' place. I'm not used to hearin' that kind of shit from you."

"You'll get over it, Lester."

"You can't drive and talk at the same time," Lester said, "maybe you should pull over on the shoulder or put the fuckin' phone away."

"Look, I'm going to have a problem with Dexter tomorrow."

"How the fuck could anyone have a problem with him?"

Danny was still behind the Honda, and the urge to slam its rear bumper into the driver's back pocket was still so strong that he slipped off the freeway at the Hollywood exit so he wouldn't be tempted any longer.

"He's going to come after me for some money," he said finally, "and I'm not going to give him a dime."

"I still don't see the problem. You think that fuckin' pussy's gonna try to strong-arm you?"

"There could be a sawed-off shotgun involved."

"He doesn't have the balls."

"Maybe not, but Louise does."

"Jeezus Christ! Is there a woman in this town that you haven't fucked over somehow?"

"Sure," Danny said, "but it's not my fault. So many women, so little time."

"This shit'll cost you extra, you want me to clean it up."

"How much?"

"Depends on how much work it turns out to be."

"I can live with that."

"And we both know you're gonna give me *my* money, don't we?"

"When did I ever short you, Lester?"

"When did you ever short Dexter? I'm just makin' sure you know there ain't nobody you can call to get *me* off your ass."

"When did you get so cynical?"

"The first time I looked in a motherfuckin' mirror," Lester said. "So how do you wanna do this thing?"

"Is one way better than another?"

"Get him out of his house. I don't want people bustin' out of closets and shit. Somewhere public is good."

"I'll get back to you."

"Do that. And here's some advice, no extra charge—fuck your fist for a while. You'll be amazed at how much it simplifies your life."

"That works for you, does it?" Danny asked.

"Go ahead and laugh," Lester said. "There ain't no bitches throwin' down on me with sawed-off shotguns."

"There aren't any bitches inhaling you like cigarette smoke, either."

"Yeah, well, you're talkin' about fuckin' the barrel of a shotgun now. How much fun is that?"

"It doesn't always turn out like that, Lester. This particular occasion is statistically insignificant, believe me."

"Fine. Just make sure you have some significant statistics in your pocket when we get together tomorrow, or you'll wish Louise had gone ahead and given you that double-barreled blow job."

"Thanks for the warning," Danny said. "And for the free advice. It was worth every penny." He cut the connection, threw the phone on the empty seat next to him, and looked around for a moment to get his bearings.

He discovered that he was driving west on Broadway, and he couldn't think of a reason to change that, so he didn't. Eventually he slipped into a parking space near the back door of a porno store and shut the Caddy down.

Somebody in there wants what I've got, he said to himself as he climbed out of the car, *and I'm about to give the mother-fuckin' faggot a mouthful of it.* Then he walked across the street and through the door, and he didn't walk back out until he had proved himself a prophet.

THIRTY-THREE

We were almost done when Leon's phone rang, me chasing the last fork in the soapy water and him waiting for it with a dish towel in his hands. We had the main floor of the house to ourselves whether we wanted it or not; the kids had vanished into the back room several minutes earlier, and the women who had ventured downstairs to eat had retraced their steps at about the same time.

Leon walked from the sink to the table in the dining room and picked up his phone. "Talk to me," he said, and then he carried the phone back to me.

"It's for you," he said. I borrowed his towel for a moment and then put Louisiana to my ear.

"This is Wiley," I said.

"This is Ronnie Jones, son. We spoke yesterday?"

"Yes, sir."

"Is there any news about our grandson?"

"I'm sorry, sir. Not yet."

"Son, is there a place we can get together?"

"Where are you now?"

"We jus' got off the plane."

"Hang on just a moment, sir," I said before I pointed my voice at Leon. "Ronnie's grandfolks are at the airport. They'd like to meet us."

"Tell 'em to come on out," Leon said quietly.

"Julie's not gonna like it."

"I know."

"How long are we gonna sit out here like this?"

"You feel like leaving yet?"

"No."

"Neither do I. So I guess the Joneses have to come to us whether Julie likes it or not."

"Sir," I said into the phone, "we're about an hour away. We'd be happy to get together if you don't mind waiting that long."

"Son, there ain't much else we *can* do at this point."

Ain't that the motherfuckin' truth, I said to myself, but I swallowed all five words so Mr. Jones wouldn't have to listen to them. What I said out loud was the address he should give to the taxi driver and a commitment to pay the fare.

"Isn't that a long ride for a taxi, son?" Mr. Jones said.

"We have a lot more money than mobility right now," I said. "It's not a problem, sir, believe me."

"All right, then. We'll see y'all in an hour or so." Then he hung the phone up on his end of the line.

"Is this the best use of our time right now?" I asked Leon as I handed him his phone.

"Beats washin' dishes," he said.

"The dishes are pretty much done. We're ready for bigger and better things."

"I know," he said slowly. "But until we can think of one of those, we might as well try to keep up with the Joneses."

THIRTY-FOUR

The sky began to drop on Danny's head as he crossed the street behind the porno store, and even after he scooted into the Caddy he couldn't escape the weight of it. He felt it pushing down inexorably on his eyelids.

"I can't believe this crap," he mumbled as he fired up the car. "I've only been out here twenty-four hours."

You're getting old, Dannyboy, he thought. *You used to put two or three days like these in a row before you ran out of gas.* He dove into his phone before he put the Caddy in gear, and a moment later the car was rolling and Rosalyn was whispering in his ear.

"What do you need, sweetheart?" she asked, a quiet rasp riding almost imperceptibly along the edge of her voice.

"A bath and a bed."

"That's all?"

"I don't have anything left, baby, believe me."

"I'll believe that when I see it, Danny."

"Just a bath and a bed, I kid you not."

"I can do a bath and a bed."

"Start the water, Roz. I'm right around the corner." Three minutes later, the Caddy was sitting under a cedar tree on Glisan Street and Danny was walking through Rosalyn's door.

Once Rosalyn got out of the way, that is, which took a while. "Straight down the hall," she said softly as she stepped aside, proving that a girl can move three hundred pounds adroitly given sufficient practice.

"You're a lifesaver, Roz," Danny said. He reached in his pocket, removed all of the money there, and extended it in Rosalyn's direction. "That's all I have on me at the moment."

She accepted his offering, scanned the bills quickly, and then buried them inside a robe he thought might have consumed enough material to clothe five or six of his regular women. At least, he thought he was thinking that until Rosalyn replied.

"Yet the whole is somehow greater than the sum of its parts," she said softly.

"Are you reading my mind?" he asked.

"Of course," she said. "Isn't that one of the reasons you come here?"

"Sometimes this is the only place I can sleep," he said. "That's why I come here."

"Uh-huh," she said. "Straight down the hall, Danny." He moved off in the direction indicated, and she trailed behind him. He opened a door when he reached the end of the hall, and steam poured out.

"Looks hot," he said.

"It is."

"Perfect." He slipped out of his jacket and dropped it on the floor at his feet.

"Let *me* do that, baby," she said from behind him, and that's what he did. Her short, pudgy fingers were soft, smooth, and warm on his skin when they got that far, and as soon as his clothes were all on the floor he moved to the side of the tub. He leaned over and tested the water with the fingers of one hand.

"Damn!" he said as he pulled his hand back. "This might be hotter than I can stand."

"Quit stalling," she said as she eliminated the space between them. "You can stand it, baby, believe me. In you go." She put one hand on his left arm and the other on his right hip and nudged him forward, and the next time he blinked he was up to his chin in water he thought might be hot enough to boil his bone marrow.

"Just lean back and soak for a few minutes. I'll be right back."

"What?" Danny asked. "Did you forget the salt and pepper?"

"Be quiet and do what you were told," Rosalyn said softly, so Danny leaned back in the heat and soaked for what might or might not have been a few minutes.

"Scoot down a little," Rosalyn eventually whispered into his ear as she gently cradled his head in both hands.

He scooted down a little, and she guided his head into the water. When she was satisfied, she said so through her fingers, and he returned to his original position. Then he stayed like that, his eyelids blissfully surrendering to the gravity of a sleepless night while she soaped and rinsed his body from head to toe—each toe, individually.

She saved the middle of his body for last, and he was almost asleep when she got there. Her soapy hands worked around his genitals so softly that he needed to open his eyes to confirm she was really there—and he didn't want confirmation badly enough to open his eyes.

"It has been a very long day," he murmured. "There won't be anything going on down there."

"Bend your knees," she whispered next to his ear.

"I'm serious, Roz."

"Hush. Bend your knees."

He followed her instructions this time because it was easier than arguing, and he soon had both knees sticking out of the water.

"Put one foot on each side of the tub," she whispered, that quiet rasp in her voice really starting to sing to him all of a sudden. She had one soapy hand massaging his penis and the other sudsing his scrotum, everything so soft he felt like he could drop into the center of it and never hit the bottom.

Then she had another hand probing even lower, which made about three hands and wasn't really possible—so Danny quit trying to keep track and just drifted with it. These were very soft hands and they asked nothing of him, so he leaned back with a foot on each side of the tub and let them slide everywhere they could reach until Rosalyn whispered again.

"Up," she said. "It's time for bed."

Damn, Danny said to himself. *She might have gotten something started there after all.* He could hear what he was thinking, but it seemed to come from the far side of a fog bank that had descended over him while his eyes were closed.

He felt Rosalyn easing him out of the tub and patting him dry with a warm towel apparently two or three feet thick. He stood next to the tub without a word until she draped the towel over his shoulders, took him by the hand, and led him back down the hall. She turned to the right and Danny turned with her, and a moment later his butt was planted on the towel and his back was pressed against a sheet almost as warm as the towel had been.

He was vaguely disappointed that sleep was reaching for him, but the hot oil started dripping over his genitals before the sleep arrived. He felt it bathing him softly for what seemed like an hour or two, and then a hand slipped between his legs and played in the slickness there until an engine started running somewhere. It was a small engine, or very far away; he could hear it buzzing persistently. And then the sound buried itself inside him, moving back and forth or in and out or up and down—he could groove on the sweet, slick rhythm of it, but he lost track of his own body somehow and could no longer differentiate bottom from top.

Then he had all of those sweet, soft hands coming at him from everywhere again, and they worked in exquisite tandem with the machine in his ass until everything exploded and melted and mercifully faded into black.

THIRTY-FIVE

"It's kinda strange seein' Junior like this," I said. I was standing in front of Julie's living room window looking out at the car Junior was using as a sentry post across the street from the house.

"Like what?" Leon asked from the couch.

"Through Julie's window, I guess. I never considered that those two worlds might overlap."

"There's only one world, bro'."

"Yeah," I said slowly. "And what a wonderful world it is."

"I agree with you there, all things considered."

"I was bein' facetious, Leon."

"I know. But you start walkin' around the house here countin' heads, and it won't take you long to see what I mean."

I didn't need to walk around the house to see what he meant, so I nodded my concession from where I was standing. But staring out the window at Junior brought back memories of the day our friend Miriam died, and I couldn't help recalling that the world had been a bit more wonderful before that day than it had been since.

"The way I remember it, we might have killed that motherfucker not too long ago."

"True," Leon said softly. "But Junior chose life that day, bro'. That's what I'm talkin' about."

I knew what he was talking about, so I nodded some more. The human race is not yet extinct because most people choose life whenever offered that choice—but I was just coming out of a long period among the minority on that question, so I knew I was still alive only because I rarely got what I wanted.

"How's Junior been?" I asked.

"If you're in full-on cynical mode, you won't believe it."

"I'm never full-on in any mode."

"He's full-time at PCC."

"Junior's goin' to college?"

"Straight through the summer, too."

"Damn, Leon. We need a thug, and you bring a college kid."

"Oh, he's still a thug. He don't have classes on Sunday."

"Dookie's probably rollin' in his grave if he can see this," I said, referring to Junior's previous employer—the one who wasn't given the choice of life on the day Junior made that selection.

"Dookie can't see shit," Leon said. "You believe anything, believe that." I nodded a little more, and I was still doing it when his phone started making noise on the coffee table next to the couch. He reached over, picked it up, did something that made the noise stop, and then told someone to talk to him, which someone apparently did for the next minute or two.

"I'm afraid it's a long story, Sam," he said finally, "and I'm pretty sure we came in at the middle of it. We won't know how it's gonna end until we find out where it started."

He paused for a moment, and I turned away from the window while he did it and locked eyes with him. "I know," he said when the moment was over. "But a little later will be a lot better than now, believe me."

That was followed by another pause, a thank-you, and a promise to keep in touch. Then he cut the connection and placed the phone back on the coffee table.

"Sam wants to know what's goin' on," I said.

"Don't we all."

"What'd he say?"

"A '67 Barracuda was jacked from the parking lot at Vancouver Mall yesterday afternoon, and it was found downtown this morning."

"Downtown Portland?"

"About four blocks from the festival."

"What the fuck does that mean?"

Leon didn't answer that question immediately. I watched him turn it over a time or two while he thought about it, and I was doing the same thing when he finally responded.

"You gotta figure they didn't walk to the mall to get the 'Cuda, right?"

"Big and Bigger? They didn't walk there, no."

"So they drove. So now they have two cars. And they don't wanna bring the 'Cuda back to the scene of the theft when they're done with it, so they drive both cars away from there."

"And they park their car downtown. About four blocks from the festival."

"Yeah," he said quietly, like he was drifting away on top of the word. "But why? Parking was a bitch down there yesterday."

"They didn't necessarily drive. Maybe someone gave them a ride to the mall."

"True," Leon said. "But the 'Cuda still ended up four blocks from the festival, and that still leaves the same question."

"Might be we're lookin' for a couple of blues fans," I said. "Or maybe the parking spot was just a coincidence."

"Yeah," Leon said. "We bein' such big believers in coincidence and all."

"Is there anything we know for sure?"

"For sure? I don't think that degree of certainty is required, bro'. We know some things for-sure enough."

"Such as?"

"They're not comin' back out here."

"On that point, certainty would be good."

"We can leave Junior here a while longer just in case, but those motherfuckers are back in Washington already."

"Washington?"

"Why pick Vancouver Mall for the car if you're not already over there? We have malls all over the place more convenient than that if you're comin' from the Oregon side."

"I guess," I said.

"But why downtown?" Leon said, more to himself than to me. "Who puts up with the hassle around the festival who ain't goin' to the festival?"

No one, I thought, and I knew Leon was thinking exactly the same thing even though neither of us said a word for a while. I turned back toward the window and stared through it while I waited for the silence to end.

"Let's say this was not a random rape," Leon said finally. "You still comfortable sayin' that?"

"Yes," I said.

"Then why'd they do it?"

"Same reasons people do anything, I guess, although a few of the usual motives obviously don't apply."

"Like love, or random acts of kindness."

"Right."

"Or revenge, I would think."

"Yeah, revenge is out. I find it hard to believe that Julie has an enemy on the face of the earth."

"So what's that leave?"

"Greed."

"Or survival."

"I doubt that Julie was a threat to the survival of those two creeps."

"I'm puttin' them on greed," Leon said softly. "And whoever's holdin' the cash in this thing was probably at the festival yesterday when Big and Bigger got paid. But whoever sent them is comin' from somewhere else—at least at this point."

"What's that mean?"

"Greed starts a lot of balls rollin', bro'."

"I get that part of it. But Julie's not a threat to *anyone's* survival, Leon."

"This ain't about Julie, remember? Maybe *we're* a threat to someone's survival."

"I think I used to know that a few hours ago," I said. "I need some sleep."

"And you knew the name of the only motherfucker on our radar screen right now," Leon said.

"Someone you might have been able to find at the festival yesterday evening."

"We get the Joneses situated, I think we need to get back down there for a while."

"Danny might be there, Leon, but there's no guarantee."

"That fat fuck who works for him will be there for sure. He's on one of the stage crews."

"Lester?"

"Yeah, Lester," Leon said softly. "For the first time in my life, I feel like talkin' to that motherfucker."

"He's more dangerous than he looks, Leon."

"Aren't we all," he said, his voice trailing off like it had somewhere else to be while I continued to stand at the window with my weary head nodding itself in agreement.

THIRTY-SIX

I walked out the front door as soon as the taxi pulled into the driveway, but both of the Joneses were already out of the car by the time I got to it. They both looked like Ronnie— or maybe Ronnie looked like both of them. They were older and significantly grayer, of course, but all three of them shared the same good looks and bodies so trim that you couldn't fry an egg if you put the excess fat from the lot of them in the same frying pan. I paid off the driver, picked up their luggage—one carry-on each, nothing extra—and escorted them through the front door.

Leon and Ronetta were waiting for us in Julie's living room. Everyone fussed over everyone else until Ronetta had the Joneses comfortably under her wing and we were out the door. After a brief detour to bring Junior up to date, Leon was easing his Mercedes down Cedar Street and I was sitting in the seat next to him watching Julie's house recede in the rearview mirror. Thirty-five minutes later, the Mercedes was resting in a parking garage near the river, and we were walking through the same festival gate I had used for my departure the previous day.

"I'm gettin' too old for this," I said as we reached the edge of the bowl already filling nicely with blues fans.

"Too old for what—blues festivals?" Leon asked quietly.

The question indicated that he had been following my comment, but his eyes gave no such clues. They were busy dissecting the crowd below us, one small slice at a time. He was starting with the north end, which was the one with music at the moment, so I started at the south end and asked my eyes to do the same thing he was doing. They didn't really want to do it, though, which was my point in the first place.

"Too old for staying up all night," I said.

"You're too old for a lot of things, bro'."

"You're the same age I am, smart-ass."

"Yeah," he said, his eyes still working carefully through the crowd. "But I age a lot better than you do."

I let that slide while I continued my survey of the scene below us. I stopped when I got to the stage Leon had started with, and he was looking at me by the time I turned my eyes in his direction.

"I don't think he's down there," I said.

"He's too old for this shit, too. He's probably crashed somewhere right now."

"Could be over by the Back Porch Stage," I said, referring to a venue for acoustic acts nestled farther north than the north stage we could see from our vantage point.

"Could be," Leon said, and he started moving slowly to our left. "Let's check in with Lester on the way."

We meandered down a long line of food booths still cranking up for the day, eyeing the people we were passing through and the crowd in the bowl now off to our right. Eventually, our path led us behind the stage where Norman Sylvester was bouncing through his set, and when we got to that point we drifted over to the knot of stagehands lounging in the area.

Lester was sitting alone three or four yards farther from the stage than everyone else, half of his big butt perched on a stool while he lined up a match with the cigarette in his mouth. He shook out the match, threw it on the ground at his feet, exhaled, and watched us approach through the smoke that poured out in front of his face.

"Those things can kill you, Lester," Leon said. He didn't say it very loud, but there was an edge to his voice that cut through the music well enough to allow us to hear every word.

"Lots of stuff like that out here," Lester said, and he must have been using the same technique because I could hear him, too.

"How much did you pay those fucks from Washington yesterday, Lester?" Leon said matter-of-factly, I think the same way he might have asked about the weather or Lester's favorite food booth. This was vintage Leon; I had seen the same ploy many times, and many of those sudden assaults managed to throw the recipient off stride a little.

It didn't work that way with Lester, though. Lester just took another drag on his cigarette, exhaled again, and stared at Leon with a blank look on his broad face. "What are you talkin' about?" he asked after a while.

"That don't ring no bells?" Leon asked.

"Should it?" Lester said.

"Be a lot better for you if it don't, truth be told."

"Gee, ain't I lucky, then."

"Maybe," Leon said, "but I doubt it."

"Where's Danny?" I interjected. "Maybe we should be talkin' to him."

"He's probably sleepin' somewhere," Lester said around a shrug and another drag on his cigarette. "I don't expect him down here today."

"If you hooked us up with his cell number," I said, "we could talk to him wherever he is."

"True, but you'd have to twist my arm pretty hard to make me do that."

"How hard would that be?" Leon asked.

"You'd have trouble gettin' a good grip, my arms bein' as thick as they are. And even if you did, other problems would ensue."

"Ensue?"

"You don't know that one?"

"Yeah, I know that one."

"You didn't think I knew it, then."

"Well, we don't really know each other, do we?"

"That's somethin' you might wanna to keep in mind."

"Likewise," Leon said.

"Look," I said, "tell Danny to give us a call when you see him."

"That I can do," Lester said, and he went back to what was left of his cigarette, and we wandered off toward the Back Porch Stage. Neither of us spoke until we walked under the bridge and through to the other side.

"You see anything?"

"No," I said. "Either we're wrong, or Lester's a lot better poker player than his boss."

"Or Lester's out of the loop on this one," Leon added.

"Yeah," I said softly. "But there's not much chance of that."

"About the same as the chances of us bein' wrong, bro'," Leon said.

"We've known Danny how long?" I asked.

"Forever," Leon said.

"Maybe we're ahead of ourselves here. I don't really see him doin' anything like this shit."

"I'm tryin' to remember the last time he walked out of my place a winner," Leon said quietly. "Our boy might be comin' apart at the seams right in front of us."

"I heard the same thing yesterday."

"No shit?"

"According to Jane Gottesman, he's not the same guy he used to be."

"I'm not sayin' the jury is in," Leon said, his voice still quiet but with a sharp edge to it that made me shiver a little, "but if any of this shit is Danny's, this is the last fuckin' guy he's ever gonna be."

THIRTY-SEVEN

"How 'bout the driver?" Leon asked. We were almost back to the Mercedes in the parking garage when he asked it.

"What driver?" I said.

"Danny's driver."

"James?"

"Precisely."

"I guess he might know where Danny is."

"And his arms aren't near as thick as Lester's, if we need to twist one of 'em."

"That, too," I said as we approached Leon's ride. "But I doubt that I could find him any faster than I can find Danny."

"I probably can," Leon said, and he ducked into his phone as soon as he unlocked his car. By the time we were both seated, he had someone on the line.

"This is Leon," he said. "I need to talk to James." Then he paused and rolled his eyes in my direction.

"You're right," he said a moment later. "So how are you? That's nice. I'm fine, too. Now give me the fuckin' number, Lawrence."

"Is there anyone in this town you don't know?" I asked as he cut the connection with Lawrence and started punching another number.

"No," he said. "But it's a small town."

"It's not that small, Leon."

"Plus I know some people better than I know others," he said to me, and then he pointed his voice into the phone. "This is Leon, James. We need to talk. Soon. Don't make me have to look for you."

"Now what?" I asked as he put the phone down and triggered something that made his seat recline.

"Now we wait," he said.

"Who is Lawrence?"

"A former flame," he said. I watched him settle into his seat and let his eyelids fall.

"I didn't know you liked 'em like that."

"There's lots of things you don't know, bro'. I might be over here lusting after your sorry ass."

"What I don't know is how you can call up somebody's former flames at the drop of a hat."

"I didn't call 'em all. I just called Lawrence."

"How do you know him?"

"Would you believe he does my hair?"

"I might, except no one but Mr. Clark has cut either of us since high school."

He turned his head a little in my direction and flashed a blind grin at me. "Lawrence does most of the repair work on my rentals," he said, his eyes still closed. "He's good—you should see that boy pound."

"Please," I said through a grin of my own. "You're killin' me over here."

"We all die a little every day. Just count this as your daily measure."

"That's the problem. Your shit comes in on top of my daily measure."

"You should thank me. Every day I trim off the end of your life is one less day of senile dementia or that mother-fuckin' Alzheimer's."

"That shit doesn't scare me," I said. "I wouldn't mind forgetting a few things."

"I think it's more of a package deal, bro'. You don't get to pick and choose."

"Figures," I said, but Leon's breathing shifted to another gear while I said it, so I knew he wasn't listening anymore. *I didn't pick the fuckin' memories in the first place,* I continued to myself, and then I leaned back in my seat and followed Leon into sleep.

THIRTY-EIGHT

It took Danny a minute or two after waking to remember where he was, but he was reminded soon enough by the lingering ache in his rectum.

"Geez, that fat bitch can fuck," he said aloud.

"I'm not a bitch, Danny," Rosalyn said. She was standing near the door, leaning lightly against the wall like she belonged there.

"That's the only part of that statement you have a problem with?" he asked.

"The rest is true."

"Please accept my apologies, then."

"Apologies accepted."

"How long have you been standing there?"

"I like watching you sleep," she said with a slight shrug.

"Now you're starting to weird me out," Danny said.

"No, I'm not."

"I stand corrected again," he said after he thought about her comment for a moment. "I like the idea of you standing there watching me, don't I?"

"Yes. You like it a lot."

"What time is it?"

"About five minutes after six."

"Do you know what happened to my phone?"

"It's on the other side of the bed there."

Danny rolled that way, picked up the phone, and began to punch in a number.

"You won't be needing anything else, then?" Rosalyn asked.

"No."

"Then I'll leave you alone," she said, and Danny was vaguely aware of her disappearing through the door as Lester's voice started grinding into his ear.

"What?" was the first thing Lester said.

"That's what I want to know," Danny said.

"Leon and Wiley were here lookin' for you" was the second thing Lester said.

"What did you tell them?"

"Nothin'. But that ain't gonna stop 'em from lookin'."

"Fuck!" Danny said, his cheeks beginning to burn on both sides of his face. "How did everything turn to shit like this?"

Lester didn't answer, but Danny skipped right over the lack of a response as his mind began to race ahead. "You said they'd be chasing their tails by now," he said.

"They were. It just didn't take very long, is all."

"What was it?"

"These two mutts from Seattle punched Wiley's ex a couple of times."

"Punched?" Danny said. "They raped her?"

"Yeah."

"Are you nuts?" Danny shouted into his phone.

"What were you thinkin'?" Lester said calmly. "They were gonna let the air out of their tires, maybe?"

"Geez, Lester. You're boxing me in a corner here."

"It's not me," Lester said. "I'm not the one who killed the kid."

"Now what?" Danny asked.

"You could beg for mercy," Lester said.

"That's not funny."

"Or you can drop 'em both before this shit spreads any wider."

"If you hit one of those guys, you better put them *both* down," Danny said softly, like he was speaking from somewhere deep inside himself. "And it damned well better stick, Lester. I don't even want to think about what will happen if either of them gets back up."

"Then don't think about it," Lester said. "Only thing you need to worry about is comin' up with the cash to pay for it."

"Pay for what?" Danny said, bouncing out of the deep quiet place feet first. "It's your ass just as much as it is mine. You aren't doing this for me."

"You like to think about it that way, suit yourself. But it *ain't* as much my ass as yours, you stupid fuck. Who hit the fuckin' nigger with the microphone stand?"

"You know what I mean. You're involved."

"Sure. I'm involved. But I get my ass in a crack, a distinction will be drawn between my involvement and yours, you can bet your sweet balls on that."

"What the fuck? Now you're threatening me?"

"There goes the language again, Danny."

"You're threatening me?" Danny said again.

"I'm not threatenin' shit. I just want you clear on who the fuck I am here."

"Who the fuck is that?" Danny asked.

"I'm the guy who gets out from under any heat that accrues by testifying against the guy who did the deed. You gettin' that?"

"Accrues? Where did that come from?"

"What? You don't know the fuckin' word?"

"I know the word."

"Then you didn't think *I* knew it. You motherfuckers are all the same."

"What are you talking about?"

"Fuck it. You're goin' into your pocket when this is done, and you're goin' in deep."

"Whatever," Danny said. "What I want to know is what's the scheme with Dexter tomorrow?"

"Don't start that shit with me, motherfucker."

"What are you talking about?"

"Don't believe what you're tellin' yourself right now," Lester said. "You'll be payin' me—you can believe that."

"All right! I hear you, for chrissakes. Now what about tomorrow?"

"Tell him he wants his money, come to my place around ten-thirty. I'll take it from there."

"Why would he do that?"

"He's the one who wants something he doesn't have yet. He'll do whatever he has to do to get it."

"Meanwhile," Danny said, "it's my butt hanging in the wind."

"You should be used to that by now," Lester said. "Just point the motherfucker in my direction and get out of the fuckin' way. And forget Wiley and Leon. The clock is already runnin' on those two."

Then Lester cut the connection, and Danny was left standing in a fat woman's spare bedroom with the empty phone in his hand and the muscle memory of her invasion of his body ringing relentlessly between the cheeks of his butt.

THIRTY-NINE

"Just tell me where you are," I heard Leon say into his phone as I climbed out of our respite. "I want to see you while we have this conversation."

"This is not a negotiation, James," he said after a brief pause. "Start talking."

"We'll be there in fifteen minutes," he said after another silent moment or two. Then he put the phone down, reset his seat, cranked up the car, backed out of our slot in the parking garage, and proceeded to beat his prediction by a couple of minutes. I had my seat back to normal and my head close to that by the time we crossed the Steel Bridge, but neither of us spoke until he pulled off Halsey into the Lloyd Center parking garage.

"He's shopping?" I said.

"Neutral territory," Leon said. "I don't think he wants me to know where he lives."

"Makes sense to me," I said. "There are times I wish you didn't know where I live."

" 'Course, you'd probably have to quit livin' in one of my houses to actually achieve that condition."

"True," I said. "Or it would be, if the condition were achievable in the first place. Seems to me you always find out whatever you want to know."

"Everyone does that," he said. "You fail to learn something, you didn't want to know it bad enough."

"I guess," I said as the Mercedes finished its climb through the parking levels and emerged on top of the garage. I could see a lot of cars at the far end near the entrance to the food court and the cinemas, but between us and them was nothing but open space and a blue Honda Civic. Leon drove his window up next to the driver's side of the Honda and stopped.

"Let's see what James can teach us," he said, and he punched a button that made the window on his side of the car disappear. James must have made a similar move, because a moment later his window did the same thing.

"Where's Danny?" Leon said quietly, but the quiet was only on the surface. Leon had a way of talking that made you hear him more clearly the more quietly he spoke.

James didn't answer right away. He sat in his car and stared out the window in front of him as if a message might come pouring through the glass if he waited long enough.

"Where's Danny?" Leon said again, this time more quietly and more ominously.

"I don't know," James said slowly, his eyes still pointed straight ahead.

"Look at me," Leon said, and James swiveled his head in our direction. "You're his driver, aren't you?"

"No," James said.

"Since when?"

"Since yesterday."

"Whose idea was that?"

"Mine."

"Why?" Leon asked, his voice still low and still with that quiet edge to it. James was looking off behind us somewhere, like maybe the answer he was waiting for might walk out of the Nordstrom store or maybe drive up the same ramp we had used to get there.

"The job wasn't goin' anywhere," he said finally.

"Why were you with him in the first place?" Leon asked.

"That I *really* don't know," James said. "I guess it sounded better at first than it turned out to be. Anyway, it's over now, and I don't know where he is."

"Can you make an educated guess?" I interjected.

"He's not alone, that's for sure. But the list of who he might be with is very, very long."

"Where does he live?" I asked.

"In the moment," James said.

"I was kinda lookin' for an address."

"He lives with his mother up in the hills, believe it or not. But all he does there is change clothes."

"His mother still does his laundry?"

"His laundry still gets done there, but his mother never had to do it."

"Sounds like he'd show if we waited there long enough."

"True," James said. "Or his office."

"Which one is more likely at this point on this particular weekend?"

"That's hard to say," James said with a shrug. "If he hasn't changed clothes yet, it's one; if he has, it's the other."

"What's his mom's address?" Leon asked. James rattled it off, but Leon looked less than satisfied with the process.

"What is it that you're not tellin' us?" Leon said.

"There's lots of things I'm not tellin' you, Leon. Where do you want me to start?"

"What do you know about Ronnie?"

"Ronnie?"

"Don't try to get cute, James."

"Oh, sure. Ronnie. What's to know about him? Hell of a bass player."

"When's the last time you saw him?"

"Beats me."

"You didn't see him when he showed up to work with Danny Friday night?" Leon asked, pitching a curve a lot like the one he had lobbed at Lester earlier.

"I wasn't there."

"You didn't pick Danny up when he left?"

"Sure, but I wasn't in the office. I can tell you the kid didn't walk out with Danny."

"Where'd you drop him?"

"Who?"

"Who the fuck are we talkin' about? Whoever you picked up."

"You got me so fucked up I don't know what we're talkin' about. I dropped Danny at some broad's place on Hawthorne."

"What time was that?" Leon said.

James was still staring off behind us somewhere, but I saw a shadow flick across his vacant eyes while he chewed on the question.

"What's the matter?" I asked.

"What?" he said, blinking a time or two as he focused on me. "Nothing. I just don't like bein' braced like this."

"Not many people do," I said. "Go ahead and answer Leon's question."

"What was it?" he asked, readjusting his gaze to focus on Leon.

"What time did you drop Danny off on Hawthorne?"

"I don't know, exactly. Two or two-thirty, I guess."

"Give me that address, too," Leon said.

"I don't know the address. It's those brick apartments somewhere across from the Safeway around Twenty-eighth."

"Which apartment?"

"Five."

"We're gonna check this out, James," Leon said. "Is that okay with you?"

"Look," James said, the shadow in his eyes suddenly a lot more than a flicker, "I said I don't really know the time. It could have been later."

"How much later?"

"I don't know, all right? Whenever the broad says it was, that's when it was, okay?"

"I'm gettin' a really bad vibe here, James," Leon said, his voice so low that it might have been seeping up to James through the air vents inside the car rather than the open window. "There's somethin' you're not tellin' us."

"What the fuck do you wanna know, Leon? My favorite color? The capitol of Missifuckinsippi? Am I a top or a bottom? What?"

"I want you to spit out whatever it is that you're chokin' on."

"It's unrelated to all this, okay? It's personal shit."

"Boy problems?"

"It never stops," he said. "It's fuckin' unbelievable."

"If I call again," Leon said, "make sure you answer."

"I will," James said. Leon hit the button again and moved his window in the opposite direction, and a moment later we were headed back down the ramp we had ascended earlier.

"What do you think?" I asked.

"Boy problems, my ass. He knows somethin' about Ronnie."

"I guess you didn't want to know what it is bad enough to squeeze it out of him."

"I already know what happened to Ronnie. I can feel it in my bones. What I want to know is where the fuck Danny Alexander is, and I don't think James knows anything more about that than what he told us."

"So where's the next stop?"

"We know three locations, and only one of them is on this side of the river."

"Hawthorne, here we come," I said, and Leon spent the next fifteen minutes making his Mercedes turn my words into the truth.

FORTY

Leon knocked on the door with the five above the peephole as soon as we got to it.

"Yes?" someone said after a minute or two.

"We'd like to talk to Danny," Leon said through the door.

"You're not the only ones," the someone said.

Leon looked at me for a moment, and I raised my eyebrows a little as I looked back. "I take it that means he isn't here," Leon said.

"That's right."

"Then we want to talk to you."

"What for?"

"Do we have to keep talkin' through the door?"

"I don't know you."

"But somehow you know you can open the door, don't you?" Leon said. Then he waited confidently until another moment of silence ticked away and the door slowly opened.

"Come in," the someone said, and that's what we did. When she motioned to a sofa nearby, we followed that suggestion, too. She closed the door, perched in a chair four or five feet from our location, and waited quietly. This threw me for a moment, until it dawned on me that she was waiting for us to finish checking her out.

Which is what we were both doing. She was a classic

blonde beauty with a lot of smooth, golden skin spilling out of white shorts and a scarlet halter. The outfit didn't leave much to the imagination, but it somehow fired up my imagination anyway.

"You must get this a lot," I said after I figured out what she was thinking.

"Yes," she said. "I guess it goes with the gift."

"In this culture, anyway," I said. "Forgive me for being another guy who fell into it."

"Sometimes it's an asset," she said with a shrug. "But this probably isn't one of them, is it?"

"Probably not," I said.

"What do you want to talk about?" she said, pointing the question at Leon instead of me.

"Dannyboy," Leon said.

"What about him?"

"What time did he get here Friday night?"

The blonde looked at Leon pointedly for a moment, as if a close examination might reveal the best response to the question. "It was more like Saturday morning," she said finally. "Four or four-thirty, I'd say. Why?"

"When do you expect him back?" Leon said, which was obviously not an answer to the blonde's question.

"So this is a one-way conversation?" she asked.

"We get a little farther into it," Leon said easily, "that could change."

"I have no idea," she said after she thought that over for a while. "He thinks that's part of his fucking charm."

"Why do you let him in?"

"That's the question of the day," she said, shaking her head slowly.

"How long have you known him?" I asked.

"About six months, I guess."

"Would you say he's changed at all during that time?"

"I don't know," she said, her brow furrowed as though she was giving the question some thought. "Do people ever really change?"

"Maybe that was the wrong question. Is there a difference in the way he acts now compared to when you first met him?"

"I don't know that, either. Most of you guys start acting different as soon as you get what you want."

"Ouch," I said.

"Maybe he's a little more hyper," she said. "More irrational; more unreliable, if that's possible. If I didn't know better, I'd think he was into drugs on top of everything else."

"Everything else?" Leon said.

"I think he's addicted to gambling, for sure—and sex, if that's possible. Can you be addicted to sex?"

"Yes," I said.

"Wanna hear something funny?" she asked. "I can't stand him, really, and I don't even like the person *I* am when he's around. Sounds kind of pathetic, doesn't it?"

"I do find it hard to fathom his appeal," Leon said.

"He's the most beautiful man I've ever seen," she said. "For whatever that's worth."

"How much *is* that worth?" Leon asked.

"That's the question of the decade," she said. "If I say not much, then what am I worth, really?"

"Do you talk like this with Danny?" I asked.

She turned her head in my direction and looked at me soberly. Her eyes were blue, but more softly so than some, and they drew me toward her without the slightest effort on her part.

"What do *you* think?" she said after a while.

"Do you know why you're talking like this with us?"

"Not really," she said, still looking at me carefully while she said it. "Because I can, I guess. But *why* I can isn't clear to me yet."

"I think it will be."

"When?"

"Soon."

"That would be nice."

"Do you know where Danny is now?" Leon asked.

"He's off fucking someone somewhere, that's for sure, but it could be anywhere."

"Do you mean that literally or figuratively?" I asked.

"That's the kind of question Danny would never ask, isn't it?" she said. "He does a lot of both. Simultaneously, sometimes."

"Sometimes?" I asked.

"He doesn't take everybody he screws to bed, if that's what you mean."

"I was thinking more the other way around."

"Is everybody he fucks screwed over, too?" she asked, her attention focused squarely on me again. "I don't really know about anyone but me, and I'm just now figuring that out."

"I already know the answer to the question," I said. "I meant it more for you than me."

She nodded slowly and turned back to Leon again. "Why are you here?" she asked.

"We need to talk to Danny," Leon said. "Do you have his number?"

"Why?"

Leon gave the question a lot of attention, and I sat back and watched him roll it around for a while. I knew what his decision was going to be, but not when he would arrive at it.

"Because we think he is *way* out of line right now," he said when he was ready.

"What's that supposed to mean?"

Leon looked over at me, and the blonde did the same. "A friend of ours turned up missing yesterday," I said slowly, "and another one was raped. We think these events are connected, and it looks like the connection is Danny."

"I would say that you have to be kidding," she said, her eyes suddenly a little rounder than they had been, "but you're obviously not."

I didn't think this comment needed a reply, so I sat there quietly and let her simmer for a moment or two. Leon apparently agreed with me, because he did exactly the same thing. She looked at me for a while, then at Leon, and when she saw what she was looking for—or grew weary of the search—she continued.

"Underneath it all," she said, "he's really not a bad person."

"We know," I said. "We have a little trouble believing this ourselves."

"It's just that there's so much fucking bullshit," she said softly. Her voice trailed off for a minute after that, and her eyes went with it. By the time she came back, she was all business.

"All I have is his message number, if that would do you any good. That and his office number, but anyone can get that."

"How well does that message number work for you?" I asked.

"Not worth a damn."

"We might as well take it anyway," I said, so she rattled it off and Leon punched it into his phone. After a brief pause, he spoke even more briefly.

"We need to talk, Danny," he said softly, but the edge in his voice was so sharp that he might have cut his own vocal cords had he been careless at all with his words. Then he disconnected his phone, returned it to the spot reserved for it on his hip, and rose from the sofa. When I followed his lead, the blonde looked at us both with a question mark on her face.

"You didn't say who was calling," she said as soon as she figured out that we weren't going to answer the question in her mind until we knew what it was.

"There won't be a doubt in his mind about that, believe me," Leon said. "Is there any doubt in yours?"

"Not really," she said, looking up at us from her perch on the chair. "I knew just as soon as I opened the door for you where I was going with Danny, didn't I?"

"Probably," I said.

"Actually," Leon said, "it doesn't matter much anymore. I don't think he's gonna be on the list of available options much longer."

The blonde blanched a little at that, but she swallowed whatever she started to say about it and stared up at us intently. We turned away, walked outside, and pulled the door closed behind us.

"Danny's gonna run," Leon said, all thoughts of the blonde behind us apparently gone from his mind. "That means the only question now is where."

I nodded in silent agreement as we retraced our steps to the Mercedes, but I could still feel the blonde's hot eyes burning a hole in my back as we walked.

FORTY-ONE

"Danny has a business here," I said as Leon pointed us toward the Hawthorne Bridge and the tony hills to the west of it. "How can he afford to just run?"

"This isn't the only place he does business," Leon said. "I think he has action all the way to Southeast Asia."

"No shit?"

"At least as far as Thailand, for sure. Maybe farther."

"What the fuck is farther than Thailand?"

"That's what I'm sayin'."

"How sure are we that he's dirty with this?"

"A little less than absolutely, I guess," Leon said slowly. "Otherwise, I wouldn't have called him."

"So you think Ronnie's dead?"

Leon nodded almost imperceptibly as the Mercedes hummed across the steel grid on the bridge, but I caught it when I looked past him to the festival spread out to our left on the downtown side of the river.

"Why would Danny do that?" I said.

"Does it matter?" Leon asked.

"Maybe not to us," I said. "But if we want to make a case to the cops, a motive would be good to have."

"Leave that shit to Sam. That's why we citizens pay his annual salary."

"If Ronnie's dead," I said soberly, "we're in Sam's territory."

"Ronetta and the Joneses are gonna handle that angle. Think of what we're doin' as a parallel investigation."

"One of these days, we're gonna push Sam too far."

"Don't worry about Sam. As long as we're righteous, he's cool with it."

"He doesn't like us constantly in his shit, Leon, no matter how righteous we are."

"True."

"And I'm not so sure we always have the same view of what's righteous as he does."

"True," he said again. "But we ain't gratuitous with this shit, are we? If we only do it when we have to, then how much fuckin' choice do we have?"

"I hear you," I said, but the lack of enthusiasm in my voice drained all the energy out of the conversation. I dropped talking in favor of watching downtown Portland march past the window on my side of the car, and ten or fifteen minutes later I was looking down on the city.

"No way," I said when Leon stopped in front of a house that might have been plucked from a glossy magazine spread if it hadn't been older than glossy magazines.

"That's the address," Leon said.

"Danny started out up here?"

"Makes for a long fall, don't it?"

"Jeezus," I said slowly. "He had the whole fuckin' city at his feet."

We sat there in the street and stared at the house until a white Lexus eased up behind us. Leon unleashed the Mercedes a little, and we climbed farther up a long block until an intersection finally gave us enough room to get out of the way. Leon U-turned after the Lexus went by, and a moment later he stopped in front of the house again.

"This isn't the place to wait," I said. Parking was prohibited on our side of the street, and the opposite side was choked with cars as far as I could see in either direction.

"I agree with you there," Leon said, and he started the Mercedes rolling again. It didn't take him long to prove Newton was right—what goes up must indeed go down. In ten minutes, we were slowly driving by the club where Danny staged most of his Portland shows.

"His office is in there, too?" I asked.

Leon nodded slightly, his eyes scanning the front of the building. I started doing the same thing, but all I really noticed was the bum pissing in Danny's doorway.

"Pretty eloquent statement, all things considered," I said as we drifted by. Leon nodded again as he dropped into one of several empty parking slots across the street and down the block from the club.

"I don't see his car," I said.

"What car is that?"

"James was haulin' him around in a new Caddy."

"Could be someone else in somethin' else by now," Leon said. "There's only one way to guarantee that he's not already here." He opened the door on his side of the car and began to demonstrate the one way he was talking about.

I got out and followed Leon's lead, and I didn't have a clue that anything was wrong until he went inside his leather jacket about halfway across the street and came out with a gun in his hand. I wasn't carrying, so all I could do was look where he was looking and try to guess which way to run.

That's what I was doing when I finally saw two big guys with brown crew cuts on the tops of their heads spilling out of a black Buick three or four spaces north of Danny's building. One of the guys was big and the other was even bigger, and both of them were pointing handguns in our direction.

The bigger of the two was on the far side of the car, his arms braced on the roof and his left hand propping up the hand holding the gun. He seemed frozen in that position for a moment, or maybe it was time that was standing still while we stared at each other, and nothing changed until Leon's gun barked in my ear and the guy's face exploded.

I hit the pavement after that, rolling hard to my right. The first thing I saw from my new vantage point was the bum in Danny's doorway diving into the puddle of his own piss, but then a bullet kicked concrete fragments in my face and I ducked my head in self-defense.

I assumed Leon was moving in the opposite direction until he sprawled on top of me. I heard four or five more shots while I struggled to regain the ability to breathe beneath his weight, and I know two or three of them came from Leon's gun because they were still thundering inside my head long after all the shooting stopped.

When I opened my eyes, I didn't much like what I saw. The big guy who still had a face was standing over us, the face twisted in a grimace built from one part each of pain and hate. His left arm hung limply at his side, and I couldn't stop staring at the blood dripping off his little finger until he moved his right hand.

I found out later the gun he was holding in that hand was relatively small, but it looked like a cannon to me at the time. I stared into the barrel of it as though close attention there might solve all the mysteries of the universe, and while I stared I waited placidly for the big bang of enlightenment.

The bang came, but I couldn't decipher the message that came with it. One moment the guy with the gun was looming above me, his grimace shifting to a grin, and the next moment the space next to my left ear boomed and the guy jumped back like someone had planted a hay hook between his shoulder blades and yanked with both hands. He sprawled backward and crumpled in a heap on the street, and then a heavy silence fell on all of us like a fog.

It took a while for my head to clear, and almost that long to realize that Leon was not moving on top of me. I had to roll out from under him to sit up, and I was able to look into his quiet eyes as soon as I did it. He regarded me peacefully for a moment, then turned his head slightly and spit a mouthful of blood into the street.

"Shit," he said softly, and then his eyes closed, the Glock dropped from his hand, and his head found a place on the pavement to rest.

FORTY-TWO

A short, slender woman dressed in green scrubs walked up to us in the waiting room. "I am Doctor Hu," she said as soon as she reached us. It sounded like "Who" when she said it, and the first thing that came to my mind was an old British television show that I once thought was funny. The next words out of her mouth kicked the visions of medical comedy out of my head.

"You are here for Leon, yes?" she asked.

"Yes," Ronetta said, rising to take the news standing up. I stayed in my chair, and so did Sam, and apparently neither of us had anything to add to Ronetta's response, because neither of us said anything.

"We are moving him to intensive care," the doctor said. "There is nothing to do for him now but wait."

"How is he?" Ronetta asked, and I had to marvel at the way she asked it. She might have been inquiring about the weather or the daily special in the hospital cafeteria.

"His condition is extremely precarious at this point," the doctor said. "On the other hand, he is a very strong man, yes?"

Yes, I said to myself, but Ronetta was the one who said it where the doctor could hear it.

"Can I see him?" Ronetta added.

"Walk with me," the doctor said. "Perhaps a quick look will be possible." Then she turned and retraced her previous steps with Ronetta in tow, and a moment later Sam and I were staring at each other for lack of something better to look at.

"I didn't know Ronetta and Leon were together again," Sam said.

"They're not," I said. "But he's still the father of her children."

"What's she to you these days?"

"The mother of Leon's children, I guess."

"I always thought you two would end up together."

"She's through with both of us, believe me. I think she likes us about as much as you do."

"Maybe you should take her somewhere besides the emergency room."

"Wouldn't help. She knows it's always right around the corner."

"If you played poker as poorly as you play your life, you would have starved to death years ago."

"I don't require much food to survive," I said. "You might be surprised at how little it takes."

" 'Course, you don't always rely on poker, do you?" This was a reference to old rumors about me ripping off drug dealers in Seattle, but those rumors had never been substantiated, and I was no longer doing it, anyway.

I didn't respond to this reference, so Sam leaned back a little in his chair, peeled the ugly black glasses off his big head, and dug a red handkerchief out of his back pocket. Neither of us said another word while he put the glasses and the handkerchief together for a while, but I could feel him shifting gears internally while he worked.

"Okay," he said as he returned the handkerchief to his pocket and climbed behind the glasses again. "Let me hear your story."

FORTY-THREE

"Isn't this where you read me my rights?" I said.

"I guess you still think you're funny," Sam said, but he wasn't laughing when he said it.

"I don't spend a lot of time thinking about it, actually."

"Don't start by obstructing my investigation. I don't need the extra aggravation."

"What's to investigate? The bad guys both died."

"Sorting out the bad guys from the good guys is generally what these investigations are all about," he said, his eyes bearing in on me through the glasses. That was one of the things about Sam—he didn't need his six feet, six inches or the 250 pounds of sculpted black muscle to intimidate most people. He could do it just as well with a hard glare through those ugly black glasses.

None of it worked on me, though, because I had been frustrating Sam since our days on opposing basketball teams back in high school. He had all that size and muscle, but I had Leon to dish to after I got Sam up in the air. I eventually grew accustomed to the frustration this caused, and so did Sam, so I just sat there in the waiting-room chair that suited me better than his suited him and waited.

"Let's hear it," he said after a while, so I started talking. When I was finished, Sam was still staring at me through his glasses like he thought the desired effect might suddenly kick in at any moment.

"Who were these guys?" he asked finally.

"I never saw either of them before."

"That's not what I asked you," he said, his glare intensifying to a degree I hadn't known was possible. I looked away to my right and watched the doors to the emergency room for a while, but the space between us continued to crackle.

"I don't know who they were," I said.

"Who called nine-one-one?"

"The bum in the doorway of the building across the street. He's the guy you should be talkin' to. He probably saw more of it than I did."

"The bum had a phone?"

"I threw him Leon's."

"Did he catch it?"

"What?"

"Did he catch the phone?"

"What the fuck difference does that make?"

"Why don't you concentrate on the answers here and let me worry about the questions?"

"Why don't you ask somethin' that fuckin' makes sense?"

"If he could catch the phone, maybe he was sober enough to know what was goin' on."

"Oh," I said.

"Well?"

"I bounced the phone off his chest."

"Then what happened?"

"He picked it up, made the call, help arrived, and here we are."

"That's it?"

"That's it."

"So Leon put the second guy down right in front of you. Did you see what happened to the guy across the street?"

"I saw his face blow up."

"You saw Leon shoot him?"

"I saw him get shot. I wasn't lookin' at Leon when it happened."

"So you *heard* Leon shoot him?"

"I heard Leon's gun go off next to me. I don't really know what he was shootin' at."

"But Leon fired the first shot."

"If he hadn't, I don't think I'd be here to tell you about it."

"And you have no idea why they were shooting at you," Sam continued, "bein' as you didn't know who these guys were."

"None whatsoever."

"Other than self-defense, of course."

"Now look at who's not funny," I said. "That's ridiculous, even for you."

"Fits all the information I have so far, Wiley," he said.

"The fuck it does. You know Leon a lot better than that."

"Are you going to tell me the rest of the story?"

"I don't know what more I can tell you."

"Why don't you start with why you guys were there?"

I had known Sam would eventually work his way to that question, which was another thing about him: He looked like a black Incredible Hulk, but his mind would have been perfectly at home in the body of a computer geek. I sat there for a moment or two before I answered, but I didn't have many choices, and we both knew it.

"We were lookin' for Danny Alexander," I said.

"So this is about the missing bass player?" Sam asked.

"I thought you didn't know what's goin' on."

"The Joneses asked me to start a homicide investigation earlier today."

"Did you?"

"No."

"Why not?"

"Homicide investigations usually start with a dead body."

"I think findin' the body's gonna be a big part of this investigation."

"In that case, their son hasn't been missing long enough to qualify."

"We knew this kid, Sam. He was as likely to miss that gig Saturday as you were to stay home the day we played for the state championship."

"So he's like that," Sam said.

"Yeah, he was like that."

"If you're right, it'll be the kid's turn soon enough. Let's get back to the bodies we already have in front of us."

"It's all part of the same story."

"Does this story have a stolen Barracuda in it?"

"Yes, but the connection is off the books."

"What does that mean?"

"Julie was raped in her house by two guys when she got back from the festival Saturday evening, but she refused to report it."

"I'm sorry to hear that," Sam said, and the way most of the hard glare in his eyes drained off somewhere while he said it made me think he meant the rape rather than the refusal to report it. The glare came back immediately, of course, but I felt it had a new target by then.

"Let me guess," he continued. "These rapists were seen waiting for her in a 'Cuda with Washington plates."

"Yes," I said.

"And they looked a lot like the dead guys I'm workin' with now."

"Yes," I said again.

"What's this Danny Alexander got to do with it?"

"The kid was working with Danny Friday night. According to Danny, he had to leave town suddenly to take care of a family emergency."

"And this is the family buggin' me to start up a homicide investigation."

"Yes," I said.

"I see," Sam said, and then he was silent for three or four minutes. I matched him word for word the entire time, but I had no idea how far apart our thoughts had drifted until he spoke again.

"So you guys had a helluva motive for wanting my dead guys dead."

"Like I said before, you know Leon better than that."

"I know he's a stone killer, Wiley. I know he'd drop the curtain on these guys faster than you and I can blink."

"Exactly," I said.

"What's your point?"

"If we had rolled up there lookin' for those two clowns, would you have found Leon bleedin' in the street when the shootin' was done?"

"There's a first time for everything. He's not as young as he used to be."

"Please," I said, and I took plenty of time saying it. "These fools jumped us, and Leon still put 'em both in the morgue."

"Who jumped who is the issue here."

"You really don't like Leon much, do you?"

"I don't like him at all."

"Well, it's clouding your view of this situation. Ask the fuckin' bum from the street who jumped whom. Drunk or sober, he'll make more sense than you're makin'."

"Whom?"

"Whatever. Don't try to change the fuckin' subject."

"I always thought you should have stayed in the classroom, Wiley. You spend too much time with Leon these days."

"Well, there you go."

"What?"

"You and Leon share that opinion. Next thing we know, you'll be seein' eye to eye with him on everything."

"How does the rape figure into this?" Sam asked, shaking his head slowly in response to my prediction.

"I don't know, really. Might have just been somethin' else for us to think about."

"So what was this shootout, then? Plan B?"

"You want me to, I'll ask Danny that soon as I catch up with him."

"Sit the rest of this party out," Sam said, his voice radiating so much heat that it almost shimmered. I made no response.

"I mean it," he said. "Stay the fuck away from it." I repeated my previous response word for word.

"I should lock your ass up right now," he added, but the life was beginning to leak from his words.

"That would slow me down a little," I said quietly, "but in the long run it wouldn't change a thing. You'd have to let me out eventually."

"I could use the time to clean this up myself," he said. "That's my job, remember?"

"He's gonna flee your jurisdiction, Sam, if he's not gone already."

"It's not that easy to get away. We don't have to stop at the county line anymore."

"I've heard Thailand, for starters."

"No shit?" he said, raising his eyebrows a little. "Thailand could be a problem."

"Not for me," I said.

"The stupid fool should have shot you, too."

"Yeah," I said as I rose from my chair. "That's exactly what he should have done." Then I turned and walked until the west wall of the hospital stood between us and the parking-lot pavement was under my feet.

FORTY-FOUR

Danny drove past Fifth when he spotted the crime-scene crowd gathered in the vicinity of his club. He parked on Fourth and walked back, picking his way through a sparse crowd of onlookers near his door.

"What happened here?" he said to a tall, skinny man looking over the top of everyone on the sidewalk.

"A failure to communicate," the man said before he tipped a bottle in a brown paper bag to his lips and sucked for a moment. "Just more of the same malevolence," he added when he came up for air.

"The philosopher king of Fifth Street," Danny said, "when all I really need is someone who can tell me what the hell came down here."

"Big shootout," the man said. "Blood and bodies everywhere. But that won't help you make sense of it, brother."

"You can say that again," Danny said.

"That won't help you make sense of it, brother," the man said again, and he followed it up with another taste from the bottle in his hand.

"What happened to the bodies?"

"Two of them left with sheets over their faces, but what will ultimately happen to them is still open to speculation."

"Geez!" Danny said. "Who the hell are you?"

"Another subject of some conjecture," the man said, consulting his bottle again.

"Did you actually see what happened?"

"The deed was done before I arrived."

"I saw the whole thing," a short gray woman interjected. "For a bottle, I'll tell you the whole story."

If I still had the price of a bottle in my pocket, Danny thought, *who knows if I'd be standing here right now.* "I'd have to go inside to get it," he said to the gray woman.

"Two guys from that black Buick there tried to take out two guys crossing the street from that Mercedes over there," she said. "They got shot to hell for their trouble."

I guess I'm good for the bottle, Danny thought. "What happened to the two in the street?" he asked.

"One of 'em got hit pretty good," the woman said. "The other one didn't take a scratch—the only one of the bunch who didn't have a gun. Life is funny, son, let me tell you."

"These guys came out of that Mercedes over there?" Danny asked, his voice a little tight around the words because he already knew the answer.

"Yeah," the woman said. "That one right there."

Sure, Danny said to himself, *the one with the fuckin' vanity plate flashin' LEON in my motherfuckin' face.* Then he stepped between the skinny man and the gray woman and threw up in the street.

FORTY-FIVE

I was leaning against the side of Ronetta's Explorer when she emerged from the building. She walked toward me briskly, and I stood there and watched her do it until she got close enough for me to watch her standing right in front of me instead.

"I thought you were already gone," she said.

"I am," I said.

"You won't be satisfied until you're in the bed right next to him, will you?" she said, the green in her eyes glinting like tiny pieces of flint.

"Nothing ever happens to me," I said. *Just to the people I care about,* I added where only I could hear it.

"Leon used to say the same thing," she said. "Now he won't be able to, will he?"

"He's gonna be fine. I can feel it."

"Even if you're right, there's always the next time."

"It's not like he brought this on himself, Ronetta."

"Really? Are you saying the same thing would have happened if the two of you had stayed out in the Grove with the rest of us?"

"I don't think that was a viable option."

"I know," she said. "You guys never do." She extracted a set of keys from the black leather bag hanging from a strap over her shoulder and put one of the keys to work, starting a series of movements that eventually resulted in her staring out of the car at me through an open window while I stared in.

"Now I get to tell his children that their daddy's shot to hell," she said. "But he'll be fine—Uncle Wiley can feel it." Then the window started up and the car started rolling, and a moment later I was standing in the warm evening air staring at an empty space in the parking lot.

FORTY-SIX

It didn't take Danny long to lurch to the top of his stairs, enter his office, clean out the safe, and collect a few odds and ends that he didn't want to leave behind. The air-conditioning had been off since the three of them had left with the dead nigger Friday night, and sweat was pouring off his face by the time he sat down to call the blonde with the pout and the perfect tits.

"Wow," she said when she picked up her phone. "I have Danny Alexander on the line."

"How do you know that?" Danny asked. "You don't have this number."

"How many people do you think have *my* number, Danny?"

"Whatever happened to 'Good morning'?"

"It's eight o'clock Sunday night. Which is not the same night you said you'd call, by the way."

"I lost a day somewhere, baby, I admit it. But I can make it up to you."

"I don't think so, Danny."

"Sure I can. I need to change the trip you booked for me, and I need to add you to it."

"Change it to what?"

"The sooner I can leave, the better. I thought we could spend a little time in Hawai'i before the Hilo show."

"That'll cost you," she said.

"Since when did you start charging?"

"I was referring to changing your flight, Danny. But now that you mention it, charging you might legitimize our relationship somewhat."

"What are you talking about?"

"The way I've been letting your treat me would be a little more appropriate if I got paid for it."

"Look, if you don't want to go to Hawai'i with me, just say so!"

"I don't want to got to Hawai'i with you."

"Fine. Then just move the damned flight, whatever the hell it costs."

"Now that I think about it, you probably have to go standby if you want to leave tomorrow. That nonstop you like fills up weeks in advance."

"What? I stand at the door every day until I get a seat?"

"The flight you booked will come up Thursday, if nothing else does."

"Forget the fuckin' nonstop."

"That's a little easier to get. But like I said, it'll cost you."

"Like *I* said, fuck the cost."

"I don't remember hearing you talk like this, Danny."

"One more person makes that statement, I'm going to fucking scream."

"What else did you want to change?"

"The return. I need to go to Singapore instead of Portland Friday. And I need a charter off the Big Island Thursday night around nine."

"What's the new return date?"

"Make it August ninth," Danny said. *Not that the date makes a difference,* he added silently.

"I'll have to go to the office to do all this."

"Would you, beautiful? Maybe you can use the time to reconsider going with me."

"I don't think so."

"Why not?"

"Are there likely to be any other women at either of those locations?"

"What kind of a question is that?"

"Maybe you should go over first and fuck 'em all. You could call me when you're done and find out if I'm interested by then."

Geez, Danny thought, but what he said was this: "When can I get the flight information?"

"Call my office in an hour."

"Thanks."

"You're welcome. But confine all of your future calls to my office, Danny."

Danny didn't bother to respond to that, except in his own head as he cut the connection and put away his phone. *One drama queen after another,* he thought. *When will this fucking shit ever end?*

FORTY-SEVEN

I don't know how long I held my position in the parking lot, but I do know that I was still standing there when Alix drove up in her Tercel and stopped right next to me.

"Thought you might need a ride," she said through the space where her window should have been. I walked around the car and climbed into the seat next to her.

"The last lady who left here wasn't likely to take me anywhere I wanted to go," I said.

"That would be Ronetta?"

"Yes."

"I'm not Ronetta, Wiley. I don't come at all this from the same angle she does."

"I know that," I said simply.

"I'm alive because you and Leon are the way you are. Fuck—my entire family is alive because of you two. I don't have a problem with the way you guys tend to operate, but that doesn't mean I don't give a fuck what you do next."

"I know that, too."

"What happened to Julie is a terrible thing. Believe me, I know what I'm talkin' about. But you can't undo it. Do you understand that?"

"Yes."

"Same thing with Leon. No matter what you do now, he still got shot today."

"I know that."

"That's all Julie and Ronetta are trying to say. There is a difference between protecting us from future harm and exacting revenge for the harm already done."

"Yes and no," I said.

"What do you mean by that?"

"I understand what you're drivin' at, but the line between the two is not always distinct. It could be that fear of the repercussions is the only reason this hasn't happened more often."

"So retaliation is actually a factor in whatever protection we enjoy?"

"Leon certainly looks at it that way."

"So do the Israelis. How safe is that philosophy making them?"

"It's kind of hard to evaluate that unless you can see the results of any alternative strategies."

"You can see how safe the place is, Wiley."

"But you can't really see why."

"If you aren't getting the desired result, shouldn't you begin to explore the alternatives?"

"Yes," I said slowly. "But the first of those may not actually be a change in philosophy."

"What else, then?"

"You can also change the severity of the retaliation."

"Jesus," she said on the front end of a long sigh. Then she stopped talking for a while in favor of looking at me in silence. I looked back the same way, but I could see almost nothing in her dark eyes.

"How is he?" she asked when she finally went back to words.

"They moved him to intensive care," I said. "I think

'extremely precarious' are the words the doctor used to describe his condition."

"I can't believe you didn't get hurt," she said.

"Nothing ever happens to me."

"Is that something you're trying to change?"

"No."

"Don't just tell me what you think I want to hear. I need an honest answer on this, Wiley."

"No," I said again. "Those days are behind me now."

"Good," she said, and I sensed something unwinding within her as she said it. Then she leaned in my direction and I leaned in hers, and we spent a moment with her forehead resting softly against mine.

"Can you promise to be careful?" she asked.

"Yes," I said.

"I guess I have to settle for that," she said before she kissed me gently on the lips and moved back behind the steering wheel. "Where can I drop you?"

"My place, I guess," I said. "I need to pick up my car."

And my gun, I thought, but for some reason—perhaps lack of confidence in my détente with Alix, or maybe just many long years of habit—I kept that thought to myself.

FORTY-EIGHT

"A funny thing happened on my way to the office, you stupid motherfucker!" Danny yelled into his phone. "You need a police pass to get to the fucking door!"

"You better hang up and dial again," Lester said.

"What?"

"You forgot who the fuck you're talkin' to."

"No such luck, Lester. I know exactly what fool this is."

"Would you lighten up? I told you we were doin' this my way now."

"And I told you not to hit one if you didn't hit them both."

"One down, one to go. And he's the easy one."

"You're underestimating him."

"Am I? What's he ever done without Leon?"

"I'm afraid we're about to find out."

"Forget fuckin' Wiley. I'm on this, okay?"

"Oh, I feel so much better now."

"That's good," Lester said. "You know whatever makes you feel better is absolutely top priority with me."

"Forget the fucking sarcasm, Lester. Believe me, I don't have time to spar with you."

"Wiley's the one runnin' out of time. All you need to do is go home, change your fuckin' panties, and practice breathing in and out for a while."

"Gee, that's a great idea," Danny said. "That's exactly what I'm going to do." *Except I'll do it out at the airport,* he said to himself, *on the far side of all those beautiful metal detectors.* "Look," he said aloud, "forget that crap with Dexter tomorrow. I'll deal with him when I get back next weekend."

"You think he's gonna sit on his ass until he hears from you?"

"You can believe I'm not going to sit on mine. All of a sudden, I can't think of a single reason to wait until Thursday to leave for Hilo."

"Yesterday you were havin' fuckin' hot flashes about the counterfeits for the Hooker show. Now they can wait until Friday?"

"I'm glad you brought that up. I'm thinking maybe we should back off of that until things settle down around here."

"Whatever. I ain't the one with the cash-flow problem."

"You worry about Wiley. I'll worry about the cash."

"Just remember the two are related," Lester said, and Danny didn't much like the edge in his voice when he said it.

"Now whose panties are too tight? You'll get your damned money when I get back on Friday."

"That's right. One way or another."

"What's that supposed to mean?"

"It means I'm not that motherfuckin' Dexter," Lester said. "I'm not even the bitch with the shotgun."

No, Danny thought, *what you are is the stupid fool I'm going to leave here holding the bag.* "Relax, Lester," he said. "Who knows who you are better than I do?"

"My problem ain't what you know, it's what you can talk yourself into when you can't *remember* everything you know."

"I haven't forgotten the first thing about you, Lester, believe me." *Which is,* Danny added to himself, *you've got the brains of a brick wall.*

"Where are you now?" Lester asked.

"I'm out at the airport," Danny said, even though the Caddy was pointed up the hill toward his mother's house as he spoke. "Why? You want to kiss me good-bye?"

"I can't believe there's a flight tonight."

"Probably not. But until you put Wiley down, I can't think of a better place to wait."

"Wiley is history. Forget that fuckin' clown."

"That's great," Danny said. "I'll go to his funeral when I get back on Friday. Now get off my phone so I can call my travel agent."

"You know it's Sunday night, right?"

"I know she's been waiting for me to call since I fucked her Friday night."

"I should have known," Lester said, his tone suddenly more congenial than before. "See you Friday, then."

If you can see me Friday, Danny thought, *you are the most far-sighted fool on the planet.* But what he said was, "Exactly," and a moment later the blonde was back on the phone.

"I got you out of here at six in the morning," she said, "but it's the scenic route."

"What's the scenic route?" Danny said.

"Alaska to Seattle, United to San Francisco, another United flight to Honolulu, and Aloha to Hilo. Thirteen hours and change."

"Geez," Danny said. "I think people can paddle there in thirteen hours."

"You should have told me you wanted to go by outrigger. I didn't look into that."

"What about the rest of it?"

"Everything's set except the hop out of Hilo Thursday night. I'll have that before you need it."

"Thanks," he said. "I appreciate it."

"The usual billing?" she asked.

"Sure," Danny said into the phone, but to himself he said this: *But don't hold your breath while you're waiting for the next check in the motherfuckin' mail.*

"Have a good trip, Danny," she said then, and something in her voice pricked him slightly as he cut the connection and triggered the opener on the door to his mother's garage.

What the fuck was that all about? he asked himself, but he didn't wait for an answer. He climbed out of the Caddy, went up the stairs to the house, and discovered the cut-down shotgun standing between him and his dash to the airport.

FORTY-NINE

"What the fuck are you doing here?" Danny said from the sprawl he was in on the kitchen floor.

"Isn't that rather obvious?" Louise said softly. She had one knee planted in the small of his back and the cut-down shotgun pressed into the notch on the back of his head.

"You're here to shoot me?"

"Don't be so dramatic," she said. "Why would I want to shoot you?"

"That's what those things are for."

"The shotgun? That's just for parity. We already know I can't outwrestle you."

"Don't even go there," Danny said. "You wanted that shit just as much as I did."

"I don't remember you cursing like this back then. I can't believe your mother would approve."

"I don't remember you coming after me with a shotgun back then, either."

"Whatever," she said. "I'm not here about that."

"What, then? The money?"

"Is there anything else between us?"

"That's between Dexter and me."

"Not anymore," she said.

"How the fuck did you get in here?"

"I borrowed the keys from your mother's cleaning service."

"What?"

"Dexter owns it. You didn't know that, did you?"

Danny didn't answer that. "So now you're into armed robbery?" he asked instead.

"No one is robbing you," she said. "You owe the money."

"I don't owe it to you."

"That's kind of a moot point, isn't it? It's not like you intend to give Dexter a dime."

Danny didn't answer that, either. "Get the hell off me," he said. "I can't even breathe like this."

Louise didn't do that. What she did instead was say this: "I prefer you the way you are. I'd fuck you in the ass first if I didn't think you'd like it."

First? Danny asked himself. *First before what?*

"Take your car keys out of your pocket and put them on the floor," she said next. "Slowly."

Danny did as he was told, and Louise leaned across him to pick up the keys. He thought for a split second about rolling with her and trying to reverse their positions, but she put more weight on the shotgun as she leaned, and the split second ended with him afraid to move a muscle.

"Now what?" he asked, after nothing happened for what was probably a moment or two but seemed a hell of a lot longer.

"Now you tell me why I don't have to shoot you before I take the money you brought from your office."

Danny felt the blood drain out of his face. "What?" he said.

"Police scanner," she said matter-of-factly, as if that explained everything. "I put someone down by the club as soon as I heard about the shooting."

"What the fuck for?" Danny asked, an image of the tall philosopher flashing through his mind. Now his face was getting hot, the blood rushing back with a vengeance.

"I thought you might do exactly what you're doing."

"Does Dexter know anything about this?"

"Dexter still thinks you're going to bring him his money after the banks open tomorrow. But he doesn't know you the way I know you, does he?"

"What do you see in that clown?"

"Nothing," she said simply.

"Then why the fuck are you with him?"

"Everyone is somewhere," she said with what Danny surmised was the slightest of shrugs, because he felt the slightest of wiggles where the shotgun rested against his head. "He's a better place to be than some I could name."

"What if I'd rather pay him than give it to you?"

"That's not one of your options, Danny," she said.

"Do any of my options allow me to get off this fuckin' floor?"

"One of them does."

"I'll go with that one."

"Probably your best choice, all things considered. I get the money from your office, you get to finish your disappearing act."

"What makes you think I had money in the office in the first place?"

"What else would you go there for? Autographed pictures of your favorite performers, maybe?"

I can't believe this fucking cunt, Danny thought, *bringing all this shit up here.*

"How did you know my mother wasn't here?" he said, his cheeks starting to burn.

"She informed the cleaning service about her trip."

"Pretty fucking thorough, aren't you?"

"Yes."

"I'm fucked either way I go."

"Exactly," she said. "But one way lasts a lot longer than the other."

"Get the fuck off me. I need to pack a bag."

She rose to her feet with the gun in one hand and his car keys in the other. It was all he could do to resist lunging at her immediately, but he managed to get up slowly and lead her through the front room and down the hall. When he got to his room he dug his traveling bag out of the walk-in closet and began throwing clothes into it.

Louise stood in the doorway and waited, her eyes locked on him and the shotgun still pointed in his direction. *Yes, you fucking bitch,* he said to himself, *but are you still fully engaged?*

"I'm wondering if you're really going to let me walk," he said as he moved into the doorway of his bathroom, grabbed his shaving kit, and tossed it on top of his clothes.

"Actually," she said, "this is my favorite option."

"Really?" he said.

"This way you're going to remember how I fucked you every day for the rest of your miserable life. I hope you live forever, Danny."

Pride goeth before the fucking fall, you stupid cunt, Danny said to himself, but what he said to Louise was this: "Can I get my hair dryer?"

She nodded, so he went a little farther into the bathroom this time and returned with a dryer in his right hand and the trailing cord in his left. He moved to the end of his bed while he wrapped the cord around the handle of the dryer, and when he was down to the plug on the end of the cord he stuck it under the last two wraps and then threw it all at the smirk Louise was standing behind in the doorway to his room.

It was over almost before it began. Louise instinctively raised her hands and ducked her head, so the hair dryer bounced harmlessly off the arm with the cut-down shotgun on one end—the shotgun now pointed directly at the ceiling. Danny came right behind the dryer, and his fist smashed into her mouth so hard she almost choked on her two front teeth when she bounced off the wall in the hallway.

Danny had both her gun and her smirk by the time Louise hit the floor. "This is really your lucky day, Louise," he said as he kicked her in the face. She slammed against the wall again, and Danny noted a new angle to her nose when she tumbled back in his direction.

"No, really," he said as he watched her try to hide behind her arms. He kicked her as hard as he could just under the point of her left elbow and felt at least one rib surrender to the impact. Then he grabbed her left arm and yanked, and she came off the floor with a scream that lasted until her face was buried in his bedspread no more than a foot or two from his travel bag.

"I'm serious," he said as he stood over her and zipped up the bag. "If I had enough time to get rid of your body, I swear to God I'd blow your sweet ass away right now."

Then Danny leaned down so he could whisper in her ear. "And don't worry about the missing teeth, sweetheart," he said. "Dexter's going to love his next blow job, believe me."

Louise moaned quietly in response to that, or maybe it was her response to the entire turn of events. "Just let yourself out when you're ready to leave," Danny said as he pocketed his keys. Then he walked out of the room with his bag in one hand and the cut-down gun in the other.

FIFTY

"Who's that?" Alix asked, referring to the old Suburban parked behind my Subaru when she pulled up in front of my house.

"Hired help," I lied.

"Good," she said. "I'm glad you're not doing this alone."

"I'll keep in touch," I said as I leaned forward to peck her on the cheek. She raised her right hand to stop me, then used her fingers to trace feathery lines down the side of my face.

"I'd like that," she said, and then she locked me up in a kiss I could feel all the way to the bottoms of my feet. We swam together in that kiss for a long time, but I eventually had to come up to breathe.

"Make sure you come back, Wiley," she said. "I'm gonna be pissed at you forever if you don't."

"I will," I said. "Hug Quincy for me."

"That's what I'm talkin' about," she said as I climbed out of her car. "You come back and do your own damned huggin'." I closed her door with a smile, tapped the top of the car, and watched her drive away before I strolled up to the driver's side of the Suburban.

"You're lucky you got here before I did," I said.

"That ain't luck," Lester said. "I ain't randomly rollin' around out here."

"One minute you try to get me shot, the next you stop by to chat? Sounds pretty fuckin' random to me."

"You turn right, one thing happens; you turn left, it's somethin' else."

"What the fuck does that mean?" I asked, and then I stood there and waited for an answer. Lester just sat there and stared at me like I was the one with the answers. After what seemed like an hour or two, he finally ended the silence.

"If those fools had actually shot you like I told them to, then you're right," he said. "I wouldn't be here. Fact is, though, they didn't."

"You could always do it now."

"Yeah, but it's not my best move now."

"I'm not so sure about that, Lester. I think I must sound a little friendlier toward you than I actually am."

"We can worry about that later. We have something else to think about right now."

"What would that be?"

"Dannyboy."

"I tend to think of you both at the same time."

"Sometimes that works, sometimes it don't."

"What's keepin' it from workin' now?"

"You," he said simply, and then he sat back again and waited while I processed that information. I worked with it for a while, but when the while was over I had yet to make much sense of it.

"I guess you're gonna have to explain it to me," I said.

"The motherfucker is peein' his pants about you right now," he said. "I don't know why, to tell you the truth, but he is. And that changes this scenario big time, believe me."

"You shoot me now, everything goes back like it was."

"It's too late. I shoot you now, I'm still not gonna see him around for a long, long while."

"It would keep me from shootin' *you,* though."

"Yeah, but then you couldn't help me run the mother-fucker down."

"Why would I do that?"

"Danny's da man here, believe me. I'm just the hired help."

"Why do you care if he runs?"

"He was gonna pay me first, I wouldn't give a fuck."

"But that's not what he's gonna do?"

"He owes people all over town. That's one of the reasons he's gonna disappear. Why would he pay me first?"

"I don't see what you need me for."

"Leaving the state is a violation of my probation," he said with a shrug of his massive shoulders. "If I go, I have to stay gone. Plus the first place he's goin', you're better suited to grabbin' him than I am, anyway."

"Where's that?"

"I point you in the right direction, you agree to come back with his cash."

"You're not payin' attention, Lester. I'm more likely to shoot you than give you a dime of Danny's cash."

"All you have to do is bring the shit back. We can argue over who gets what then."

"You don't sound too worried."

"Why should I be? You don't wanna share it, I'll take it all."

"Wouldn't that be a violation of your probation?"

"I like my chances of keepin' my PO from findin' out about that one."

I took a break from staring into Lester's quiet eyes at that point in favor of looking blankly at the front of the Suburban while I pondered our conversation. It struck me as totally sick, but I found myself drawn to the irony intrinsic to it.

"I can do that," I said after a moment or two, "but I still don't see why you want me to."

"He's goin' to Hawai'i," he said, making it sound like Ha-why-ah when he said it.

"So?"

"So you're Hawaiian."

"You have no idea how funny that statement is. I've never even been there."

"Look, he's got guys like me with guns over there. I hop a plane, I won't have shit when I get there."

"You think I have a special pass of some kind?"

"What you have is a much better chance than me of comin' up with somethin' once you get there."

I started to laugh out loud at that, but the energy drained out of the effort at the last possible moment. I suddenly remembered the Samoan cab driver from Hawai'i I had met the previous year in Las Vegas, and I realized Lester might be right.

"The people I know might not have the kind of connections you're talkin' about," I said.

"Bad as he seems to think you are," he said, "you might be able to scare the money out of him without a gun."

"Yeah, right."

"Look, whatever your connections are, they're better than the ones I don't have."

"Why don't you put an arm on him before he leaves?"

"Fuckin' nine-eleven."

"What?"

"Fuckin' terrorists made a no-touch zone out of every airport in the country. If he's not out there already, he's on his fuckin' way."

"If that's the case, what's gonna make him come back here with me?"

"I don't give a fuck if *he* comes back. All you have to bring with you is his cash."

"That's not good enough for me."

"Then you do whatever you gotta do. That's none of my business."

"It will be when I get back."

"Yeah. That's what you keep sayin'."

"Just so you know."

"I take care of whatever *is* my business, Wiley. Just so *you* know."

"Why don't I just point my homicide friend at him? Airport security is no problem for him."

"Neither of us gets what we want that way. The cops won't have anything to hold him with without me, and once they let him go he'll really be gone."

"You could always give him up."

"Before I get paid? You're the one ain't payin' attention here."

Actually, he had my full attention, and he knew it. I chewed on everything I had gleaned from the conversation for a while, but it became no easier to swallow in the process.

"When is he supposed to be in Hawai'i?" I asked.

"He has a show in Hilo Thursday, but I'm sayin' his time of departure is gonna move forward dramatically."

"If he's as spooked as you think, why would he sit over there and wait for me? Or you, for that matter. He's probably seen you violate your probation before."

"He thinks I'm stupid," he said with another quiet shrug, "and that you won't know where to look."

"Too stupid to know he owes you money?"

"Too stupid to know he's not comin' back on Friday. He already gave me a song and dance about leavin' early, and right now he expects to laugh all the way to fuckin' Gookville about it."

"Is there any chance he'll skip the show in Hawai'i and just keep right on goin'?"

"Long as I sound like I'm swallowin' his fuckin' shit, he'll think he has plenty of time to rip off those fools, too. Keep that in mind if you try to intercept him there—he won't be around when that show ends."

"Do you realize how fuckin' sick this conversation is?"

"Whatever. This is still your best move right now."

I shook my head slowly, but it was a signal to myself more than to him. "You're absolutely right," I said softly. 'That's what's so sick about it."

"Guess I better run like hell once you go in the house," Lester said.

"I wouldn't look for a lot of repartee the next time we meet," I said.

"You bring the money, I won't miss the small talk."

"What makes you think I'll bring the money in the first place? I'd rather give it all to the Salvation Army than let you have any of it."

"That's the one thing I've heard about you I actually believe," he said quietly. "You'll bring it because you said you would."

I locked eyes with Lester instead of responding, but I could have stalled for twice as long and still not come up with a decent denial.

"Don't believe everything you hear," I said as soon as I gave up trying to think of something better. "It's human nature to exaggerate." Then I walked between his car and mine and headed up the driveway toward the back door of my house.

"Wiley," he said when I was halfway there, "the people I been talkin' to ain't all that human." I stopped and turned in his direction, but he was rolling into the street by the time I did that, and I had nothing to respond to but his receding taillights—plus the voice in my own head asking me questions about what I was doing that I couldn't begin to answer.

FIFTY-ONE

I entered my house through the back door and walked straight to my computer, and my first decision was behind me by the time I sat down in front of the screen.

I selected Thursday evening at the show in Hilo for my rendezvous with Danny for two reasons: It saved me from hunting for him in a place I knew nothing about, and it gave me a few days to nurse Leon out of intensive care before I had to leave.

My head began to hurt before I got to the bottom of my second decision. It only took me three or four minutes on the computer to find a combination of three jets that would get me to Hilo by showtime, but the return flight was another proposition altogether.

I used to teach my high school students about the limitations of force during my former lifetime—back when I still thought knowledge could set a person free rather than bury him alive—and the problem of getting Dannyboy back to Portland was a classic example of my thesis. Force can be used fairly effectively to *stop* people from doing something, but it is much less reliable as a way to *make* people do something. Anyone who would rather die than cooperate, for example, can't really be forced to do shit.

I didn't think Danny was in any hurry to die, but I

couldn't see a way to force him back to Portland as long as we needed an airport to get there. That's where the headache came in, because this kind of thinking made me admit that the limitations of force would once again apply: It would be a lot easier to stop him from leaving Hilo than to make him go anywhere.

I put off the resolution of this quandary by ordering a one-way ticket to Hilo for myself, but I knew the ultimate decision was still out there waiting for me. That's what was making my head hurt, which was further evidence of my new thesis: Ignorance really is bliss, whereas knowledge frequently hurts like hell.

Nofo was next on my list of things to do, and the call to him in Vegas came with its own kind of hurt. I used the number he had given me the previous year as one Polynesian on the wrong side of the Pacific to another, and he answered it with a musical hello on the second ring.

"This is Wiley," I said, and then I didn't say anything for a moment while I waited to find out if my name still meant anything to him.

"No sheet!" he said. "How you, brah? And Miriam—how she?" The reference to Miriam was the part that hurt, because Miriam had been shot to death just a few days after Nofo taxied us from Vegas to L.A. If we had followed his advice at the time, we would have gone from there to the islands instead of Portland, and Miriam would have survived that terrible week.

"She died," I said simply.

"Fuck," Nofo said, and he let that single word say it all for a silent moment or two. Then he added on a few more. "Da guy was chasin' you in Vegas?"

"Yes."

"Should have gone to da islands like I tol' you, brah."

"I know."

"Now you gonna tell me you nevah make it ovah dere yet."

"I'm goin' to Hilo Thursday," I said. "That's why I'm callin'."

"Dat's somet'ing, brah. I gonna hook you up with some people you wanna meet."

"This isn't a social visit, Nofo. What I need is a reliable handgun after I get there."

I heard no response to that for several heartbeats, and it wasn't for lack of trying on my end. My effort was finally rewarded, but only briefly.

"Fuck," he repeated, and then the sound drifted away from our conversation again. When it finally returned, I wasn't immediately certain it was worth the wait.

"Why you t'ink I can hook you up like dis, brah?" he said.

"I don't think you can," I said. "I just hope you can. I don't have any other possibilities."

"You got one Hilo problem?"

"No," I said. "It's a Portland problem gonna run to Hilo."

"Dat's good da kine, but I still got plenty worries."

"What?"

"Guns kill, brah, and I care da kine get killed."

"You don't care about this one, believe me."

"Guns start poppin', lotsa people can get shot."

I didn't really have a reply to that, so I waited for him to say something else. What he finally said was this: "Give me one numbah and hang tight. You gonna get a call pretty soon tell you wheah to go."

"I appreciate this more than I can say, Nofo."

"Hope you still feel dat way when it's ovah. You got me plenty worried now, brah."

"Don't be," I said. "Nothing ever happens to me."

"What happened to da guy did Miriam?"

"She shot the motherfucker pretty much to death," I said.

"Miriam did dat?" he said, as if he couldn't quite believe it.

"Yes, she did."

"Better den not'ing dat way, right?"

"I guess so."

"You bettah believe it, brah. But don't you do da kine—I gonna be pissed, I promise."

"Thanks, Nofo," I said, then gave him my number and hung up the phone. Just shy of thirty minutes later, I had pickup instructions in my shirt pocket and my butt in the seat of my car, and four or five minutes after that I was sitting in the waiting room at Emanuel in front of a sign that read INTENSIVE CARE.

FIFTY-TWO

Danny was driving east on I-84 when it came to him that the airport could wait a few more minutes. *What could stopping for a quick jump possibly hurt?* he said to himself. *I sure as hell don't like my chances of coming up with one at the airport.*

It didn't take him long to follow through on that line of thought. He nosed off the freeway at Eighty-second and had the Caddy parked in back of the same jack shack he had visited the day before almost as fast as he could sing "Cherry, Baby!"

Some of the air escaped from his sails when he found out Cherry was not on the premises, but Kiki's efforts to distract him from that disappointment met with immediate success.

"Is that good or bad?" she asked.

"What?" Danny said.

"The fact that I'm not Cherry. With me, you don't have the comfort of the familiar. But you do have the thrill of the unknown."

"Good point," Danny said as he looked Kiki over. He had to look through a blue negligee to do it, but it was a filmy blue that didn't put up much of a fight. He could see that she was a little thinner than he liked, but she still seemed to bulge intriguingly in all the right places.

"I have everything Cherry has, I promise," she said.

"It's not so much what she has that I like," he said. "It's more what she's willing to do with it."

Kiki made the space between them disappear, and then she wrapped one arm around his neck and drew his left ear all the way down to her lips. "Step into my office, Danny," she whispered. "I can't think of a thing I'm not willing to do with you."

"My pleasure," Danny said.

"Exactly," she said, her lips barely brushing against his ear as she spoke. "I just need forty dollars for the boss to get this started."

Danny fished a fifty off the new roll in his pocket. "Right this way," she said as she took the bill and the hand holding it. She led him down a short hallway and ushered him into a small room furnished primarily with a padded armchair and a thick white towel.

"You can take off your clothes, Danny," she said, "but don't you dare start without me." She darted back down the hallway while Danny entered the room, closed the door, and started shucking garments. By the time Kiki returned with his change, he was sitting in the chair with his erection in his right hand.

"Danny!" she said. "I told you not to start without me!"

"You haven't missed a thing, believe me," he said.

"This is yours," she said, handing him the ten in her hand.

"There's a lot more where that came from."

"That's good," she said simply, but the way she was eyeing the cock in his hand he wasn't sure she was talking about the money. Then she said, "Shoo!" and brushed his hand away.

"You like?"

"Oh, Danny! If you only knew how we girls talk!"

"Please," he said, but he loved this turn in the conversation and they both knew it.

"I swear to God, Danny! Cherry's got us all itchin' for a chance like this."

"Aren't you the lucky one, then."

"Exactly," she said. She stepped across the room to a CD player Danny hadn't noticed before and pushed a button, and by the time the filmy blue negligee got completely out of the way Marvin Gaye was also in the room.

"You have better taste in music than Cherry," he said.

"That's just the tip of the iceberg, Danny. Cherry's about to lose her favorite customer."

"What's this going to cost me?"

"You're a gambling man, right? How about double or nothing?"

"What?"

"You give me double what you give Cherry if I'm better than she is. If I'm not, you don't have to give me a thing."

"What makes you think I'll tell the truth?"

"By the time I get through with you, Danny, you won't have nothin' left in you *but* the truth."

"Prove it," Danny said, and Kiki did.

FIFTY-THREE

Geez, Danny said to himself as he left the building, *that girl can really go!* He rode the buzz from where Kiki had gone all the way down the short flight of stairs and across the parking lot, but it dissipated immediately when Dexter climbed out of one side of the car next to the Caddy and a Mexican-looking motherfucker emerged from the other side.

The motherfucker walked around Dexter's Lexus and lit Danny up with a hard right to the gut. Danny fell all over the punch, and as soon as he hit the pavement he got a sharp kick in almost exactly the same place for his trouble.

"You are so fucking predictable, Danny," Dexter said, pushing his bifocals a little farther up his nose with the index finger of his right hand. "Louise knew exactly where you'd be."

"I didn't think that fucking bitch could still talk," Danny said, but he was having a little trouble talking himself.

"She's a little hard to understand, it's true. But she was determined to get the message through."

"Did she tell you she tried to rip you off?"

"Yes," Dexter said, "and I was none too pleased to hear it. But I gather she has already paid dearly for that transgression, hasn't she?"

Not nearly dearly enough, Danny thought. He looked up at

Dexter and then at the Mexican-looking motherfucker, but they were both staring down at him like no one knew the next item on the agenda.

"Give my money to Hector, Danny," Dexter said finally.

Danny rolled up on his hands and knees and began to retch, but nothing came up but waves of pain. The retching stopped after a while, though, so Danny eventually climbed to his feet, came up with the keys to the car, and opened the trunk.

"There's more here than I owe you," he said as he handed Hector the bag from his office.

"I doubt that, Danny," Dexter said. "You owe me a lot more now than you did before."

"That's what I thought you were gonna say," Danny said as he went back in the trunk for the cut-down shotgun, pointed it at Hector, and pulled the trigger. When nothing happened, he worked through the shock faster than Hector did. He started beating the motherfucker in the face with the thing, and he didn't stop until Hector was sprawled on the pavement with no visible signs of bounce.

Meanwhile, Dexter stood there and watched it all like his eyeballs were about to pop. "You are one lucky sonofabitch, Dexter," Danny said as he picked up his bag, returned it to the trunk, and slammed the lid shut. "If this piece of shit had worked, you and Hector would both be dead right now."

"What happens next?" Dexter said, although he had suddenly joined the can't-talk-that-well crowd by the time he said it.

"Give me your keys," Danny said, and Dexter leaned into the Lexus and came out with the keys.

"If you come after me again," Danny said as he snatched the keys, "you'll need a fucking army of Hectors to keep Lester off your sorry ass. Do you understand me?"

Dexter didn't say anything in response, but his bifocals

moved up and down, so Danny took that for an affirmative answer. Then Danny walked around his Caddy, climbed in, and cranked it up. He rolled out of the parking lot and nosed the car northward as soon as he caught a break in the traffic. Somewhere in that sequence he caught a flash of Dexter kneeling over the Mexican-looking motherfucker in the parking lot, but Danny didn't give the sight a second thought.

Instead, he winced as he drew in a deep breath and thought this: *Never used to be* this *goddamned hard to get laid.*

FIFTY-FOUR

It turned out that Leon had been lucky—or as close to that as someone can be who had been shot almost to death in the street. Luck was nothing new for Leon, though, and I had been counting on that characteristic to carry him one more time.

Actually, Leon's luck is one of the things I had always hated about him. He seemed to have unlimited access to it, while the rest of us were all out there fighting for the leftovers. On that occasion, however, I had been rooting with all my heart for his luck to hold, and that's exactly what it did—twice, in fact.

For starters, he had been shot by the right shooter. I found out from Sam that Big and Bigger described not only our attackers but also the guns they were carrying, and the slug that nicked Leon's lung came from Big's .22 rather than Bigger's .45.

As usual, Leon would not concede that this was luck when we discussed it later. "I shot the motherfucker with the forty-five before he could fire the fuckin' thing, remember?" he said.

"That's what I'm talkin' about," I said. "You were lucky."

"If you shoot the lion before you shoot the monkey, is it luck?" he asked, shaking his head like he didn't have the energy to explain the basic facts of life to me again. Which was fine with me, because I didn't have the energy to listen to the explanation again.

However, even Leon couldn't argue the second example of his good fortune: the fact that Dr. Hu had been the surgeon on call when he rolled into the emergency room.

"*That* was lucky," Leon agreed when I brought the subject up. This was after we had heard from several sources that the Chinese doctor had serious game when it came to emergency surgery.

None of this happened immediately, of course, because I saw Leon for three days before he was able to see me back. I had to skirt the rules of the hospital to do it, but I didn't mind the absence of perfect access because I couldn't take much of looking at him like that anyway. We've all seen enough hospital-room dramatizations on screens big and small to know what to expect, but it's still hard to be sanguine about the scenario when the star is your oldest friend in the world.

Leon wasn't quite himself when we finally got to talk. He seemed smaller, somehow, and paler, too—like some of the pigmentation had poured out of his skin with the blood. Plus he was flat on his back with hospital equipment running in and out of his body in several directions, which was a long way from his usual taste in accessories. Still, his eyes had their customary quiet confidence, and they smiled when he saw me even though his face did not.

"How you doin', bro'?" he asked softly.

"That's my line, isn't it?"

"Everyone knows how I'm doin'," he said. "You're the one ain't hooked up to health monitors."

"I'm always fine."

"Or never. I'm not sure you can tell the difference anymore."

"I can tell I'm still alive," I said, staying as far from his statement as possible. "I want to thank you for that."

"Why don't you do me a favor, instead?"

"Name it."

"Let this shit ride for a while."

"What?"

"Back off this thing with Dannyboy."

"Why?"

"This shit was never your game, bro'," he said softly, closing his eyes and settling back in his bed as he said it. "It ain't what you're supposed to be doin'."

"What I'm *supposed* to be doing? Now you're starting to sound like Mrs. Boomer, Leon."

"Exactly," he said.

"What makes you think I'd let either of you tell me what I'm supposed to be doing?"

"Nothin', bro'," he said, bringing his eyes back into the fray. "That's why I asked you to do it as a favor to me."

He gave up words for a while then, as though he had only a limited supply, and I followed his example even though I did not suffer from the same condition. I sat there next to his bed and stared into his quiet eyes, and he lay back and let me do it. I felt like I was looking into my own head rather than Leon's, though, and what I saw gave some credence to what he had been saying.

"You're not sounding like yourself, Leon," I said finally.

"This ain't about me."

"I'm not so sure we're that different from each other."

"Which one of us had a gun in the street the other day?" he asked. "This is my kind of shit, bro', not yours."

"Maybe," I said slowly. "But we were both in the street, weren't we?"

"Yeah," he said, his eyes shutting down again. "But you didn't belong there."

"I don't really belong anywhere, Leon. That street seemed

more appropriate than anywhere else I might have been at that moment."

"Things ain't always what they seem to be, bro'."

"I know," I said, my voice almost as weary as his. "But we still have to go with what we know at any particular moment, right?"

"True enough," he said. "Except we deny some of what we know some of the time, don't we?"

I didn't answer that, but it was only because we both knew the answer already. A couple of silent moments limped by until he spoke again.

"What's the plan?" he asked.

"I'm leavin' for Hilo tomorrow," I said.

"Hilo?" he asked. I nodded, and he cracked a pained smile as I did it. "I always wondered what it would take to get you to the islands."

"Well, now you know."

"You're gonna have some trouble gettin' him out of there, bro'."

"I know."

"Might not be possible, actually."

"I know," I said again.

"Then what?"

"I have no idea."

"That should work," he said with another grin, and this time I couldn't tell if it hurt him to smile or not.

FIFTY-FIVE

My first flight to Hawai'i did include a homecoming of sorts, but the round brown woman who welcomed me home in Hilo didn't quite get it right. My hometown was San Francisco, and thoughts of that city and its place in my life flooded my mind during the first leg of my trip to the Big Island.

This took some mental agility on my part, however, because I had no memories of living in San Francisco. My experience was apparently the reverse of Gertrude Stein's, the infamous wit who put Oakland down by saying, "There's no *there* there." For me, that description fits Stein's beloved City by the Bay a lot better than it fits Oakland.

The single most important event in my childhood occurred in San Francisco, but it happened when I was only two or three and consequently lurks wherever we store everything that happens before our memories engage. Not that it was about me, anyway. It was actually about the adults in my life: the stepfather who crept into my family while my father was gone at sea, the mother who let him do it, and the father who walked away from the whole mess as soon as he got back to town. So I ended up with no memories of San Francisco or of my short life with my father, but far be it from me to complain. After all, I have crystal-clear recollections of Oakland and the motherfucker who moved us there to sustain me.

My mind drifted in a different direction during the long flight from San Francisco to Honolulu. This was uncharted territory for me, but all I could think about along the way was ground I had covered many times before.

I had killed three men during the past two years, but I was not yet accustomed to that fact and not at all comfortable with the idea of adding anyone to the total—especially not Danny and not even Lester, who clearly deserved that fate just as much as the others.

It wasn't that I suddenly started thinking those dead men should have gone on living. The way it had come down, *I* would have died had any of them continued to live. But I had to admit that Ronetta and Julie were right, in a way— Leon and I had a lot to do with the way that had all come down.

Maybe we were just self-fulfilling prophecies, as Ronetta and Julie believed. I was certainly in the process of dictating how the thing with Dannyboy was going to come down. The choice would ultimately be his, of course, but I was the one who would force him to choose. And I already knew what his choice was going to be, which is why I had lined up a gun long before I arrived in Hilo.

Because of thoughts like these, I had no fear of what might occur once I caught up with Danny. What I felt instead was a sadness so deep that it almost took my breath away, a dark melancholy related not to the lives I had taken, really, but to the lives that had been taken from me—except that all of these lost lives, deserved and undeserved, suddenly seemed like petals ripped from the same poisonous rose.

My mind jumped again on the short hop from Honolulu to Hilo, so by the time I landed there I had to admit that my last affirmation to Alix had been a lie. Or maybe an inadvertent inaccuracy, just in case I had been telling the truth at the time. Either way, my mindset when I accepted the gun from the Samoan in the KFC parking lot was firmly within the old reality I had assured Alix was far behind me. I had returned to that frozen place where I didn't give a fuck what happened next as long as I dictated the choices.

If Danny decided to come back to Portland with me, fine: I'd turn the whole fucking mess over to Sam and let him do his job. If Danny refused, that was fine, too: One of us would join the dearly departed, and one of us would wait for a later flight. By the time I parked my rental car within sight of the Civic Auditorium in Hilo, I was no longer perfectly sure which of the two I preferred.

FIFTY-SIX

I had a lot of time to think while I was staring at the side of the auditorium, but every thought that crossed my mind eventually curled around to the woman I had met in the bookstore.

I was finally in the place where my father had been born, but I could have been anywhere on the planet developed enough to have a Wal-Mart, a KFC, a shopping mall, and an auditorium with a parking lot. The rain was warmer and the palm trees more plentiful than in Portland, for sure, but I could have been in Miami rather than Hilo—except for the fact that Hilo could be stuck in Miami's back pocket, of course.

And except for the woman with the scar on her face, who resonated *Hawai'i* out of every pore in her brown skin; and except for the people who had hooked me up with a rental car; and except for the guy with a gun in a bag who was probably more Samoan than Hawaiian but had plenty of resonance to spare.

My head was swimming with recollections of the conversation in the bookstore when the limo arrived. I saw it at 8:35, and I was walking from my ride to Danny's by 8:36. That's counting the time it took me to stash my thoughts, go into the athletic bag in the trunk of the rental car, and come out with the gun. I stuck the gun inside the waistband of my slacks under my aloha shirt and then began putting one foot in front of the other.

The rain had stopped by then, but the music had not. The Coasters were romping through "Charlie Brown" as I approached the building. Somehow "you're gonna get caught, just you wait and see" seemed like the perfect setup for the next scene.

The limo was parked along my side of the auditorium by the time I got there, and the driver was leaning against his door while he set a wooden match on fire with his thumbnail and brought the flame to the end of a Lucky Strike.

"Where the fuck do you find those?" I asked. "I haven't seen Lucky Strikes since I was a kid."

"Ain't easy," he said as he took a drag. He was about as tall as his car but much thinner, with a gnarled face that had probably originated on an island chain closer to Asia than Hawai'i.

"Haven't seen wooden matches for a while, either," I added. "Everyone on the mainland has switched to fuckin' Zippos or Bics."

"Same t'ing heah," he said, smoke swirling out around the words when he said it. He eyed me through the smoke, and I stood there for a moment or two and let him do it. Finally, he said this: "You look mebbe local, but you no soun' da kine."

"It's a long story," I said as I peeled a hundred off the fold of bills in my left front pocket.

"Ain't dey all," he said, but by then his eyes were focused on the money in my hand.

"I'd like to buy your next carton," I said.

"Ain't *dat* hard to find, I promise," he said with a short laugh.

"And the matches, too," I said, and he laughed a little more at that. "Plus I need to wait inside your ride until your client comes out."

He stopped laughing then, but he took the hundred out of my hand and opened the passenger door on our side of the car. I slipped in, and he closed the door behind me, but I had to dig the gun out of my pants before I could settle into the plush seat cushions.

The gun looked a lot like Leon's, which I understood to be a nine-millimeter Glock. I don't know shit about guns, but I fumbled around with that one until I had some hope that it was ready to fire. Then I found a button on the door that might lower the window and pushed it.

"Where are you taking this guy?" I asked as soon as the window did what I wanted.

"Airport," the driver said.

"You got flights out this late?"

"He got one chahtah."

"That'll work," I said, but the driver noticed the Glock in my lap as I said it, and that sent the conversation in a slightly different direction.

"Don't shoot no one in my cah," he said. "Gonna need plenty mo' da kine what you wen give me, you gonna do dat."

"Anything happens in your car, I'm good for it," I said, but I lost interest in the sentence about halfway through because a pair of human bowling balls wearing polo shirts with the word SECURITY plastered across the front popped out of a side door of the building. They looked around from the doorway for a brief moment and then stepped aside, and Danny Alexander strolled out with a leather satchel in one hand and a cell phone in the other.

FIFTY-SEVEN

Danny was only three or four steps from his ride when he came out of the building, but by the time he got to it the driver had flicked his cigarette into a puddle, circumnavigated the car, and opened the passenger door. Danny clipped his phone to his belt as he climbed in, so he didn't notice that he wasn't alone until he was more in than out.

"Keep right on comin', Danny," Wiley said. He was holding a gun up where Danny could see it in the glow of the light that had come on when the door opened. Danny froze for an instant, thinking this: *What the fuck is this shit?*

When the instant ended, Danny finished entering the car. The driver closed the door behind him and the dome light went out, but Danny had no problem seeing the gun in the dark.

"Those security dudes should have walked you to the car." Wiley said.

"Fucking Polynesian niggers," Danny said as the car started to roll. "It's a real bitch getting competent help over here, believe me."

"I guess paradise isn't everything it's cracked up to be."

"Oh, it has its attractions, Wiley, don't get me wrong."

"I'm really relieved to hear it."

"Oh, yeah," Danny said. "The women really love to fuck,

for one thing. If you catch them young enough, it's even worth the sweat off your balls to do it."

"You tryin' to hurt my feelings, Danny?"

"All I'm trying to do is figure out what the fuck you're doing here."

"Is it just me, or are you swearing a lot more than usual for you?"

"Don't even go there, I'm warning you."

"Shouldn't take you long to figure out what I'm doing here, Danny."

"I guess you've been talking to Lester."

"What makes you think that?"

"Someone had to tell you where to go."

"Lucky someone did," Wiley said. "You became kinda scarce all of a sudden."

"Look, you can't believe a thing that fat fool says."

"You did scoot out of the concert just like he said you would, Danny. It's a shame you couldn't stay for the rest of the show."

Been there, done that, Danny said to himself, but what he said to Wiley was this: "Can we cut the crap? You're here with a gun, so you clearly have the whole wrong idea about what's going on."

"You wanna cut the shit," Wiley said, "you're gonna have to clean up your end of this conversation."

No, old buddy, Danny thought as the limo turned left where Manono intersected with the road to the airport. *What I have to do is keep this shit going until we get to the fucking plane.*

"Look, Lester's completely around the motherfucking bend," Danny said. "The crazy fool thinks I owe him money for cleaning up the mess *he* made!"

"What mess is that, Danny?"

"The fucking kid, what else? Lester clocked him with a microphone stand right in my fucking office!"

"Why?"

"The kid scoped out Lester's counterfeit ticket scam. He said he had no choice but to report it, so Lester lowered the boom on him."

"And Lester probably sent the guys who raped Julie out in the Grove, too."

"This is the first I've heard about that, Wiley. Come on, does that sound anything like me?"

"And the thing in the street by your office?"

"That's when I knew it was time to cut and run. I'm telling you, Lester has completely lost his mind."

"That's why you need to hurry on back to Portland," Wiley said. "Be good to get the truth out about the situation."

"It's not quite that simple," Danny said as the limo stopped at the light on Highway 11, but he was thinking this: *Just a couple more minutes, my friend.*

"That's right," Wiley said. "There's the thing about the money you have in the bag there, and the money you owe back home."

"I'm not going to lie to you," Danny said. "My ass is hanging in the wind, I admit it. I can't really go back to Portland right now."

"And you can't really stay here now, either."

"That's right. I admit that, too. But all that has nothing to do with you, Wiley. You need to go back and talk to Lester again."

"That's the very next thing on my list, Danny."

"After what? You came all the way over here to shoot me, is that it?"

"If that's the way you want it."

"That's not the way I want it," Danny said. "Let me clear that crap up right now."

"Good," Wiley said. "That's not the way I want it, either."

And that isn't the way it's going to go, Danny added to himself as the limo finally caught the light and crossed the highway, *which you are about to fucking find out.*

"So you're going to walk me all the way back at gunpoint," Danny said. "Is that the plan?"

"Would that it were, Dannyboy."

"What's that supposed to mean?"

"I could do it that way, I'm pretty sure you'd make it back alive."

"You can dial down the drama, Wiley. You've got me and Lester totally confused here, I'm telling you. There's no fucking way I'm dying over this shit."

"I take it you have a charter to Honolulu tonight?" Wiley asked as the limo veered to the left short of the main terminal.

Yeah, Danny said to himself, *and I'm going to be on it in the very near future.* "Yeah," he said aloud.

"You can't add me to it, we're gonna have to cancel it."

"That's not a problem," Danny said.

Then the limo eased to a stop. The driver got out, walked around the car, opened the door next to Danny, stepped aside while Danny and Wiley climbed out, and then hammered Wiley's left temple with a fist full of dimes. Wiley went down like he'd been chainsawed at the knees, and Danny kicked him squarely in the face.

"No make him bleed!" the driver said sharply. "Gonna be pissed he mess up da cah, I promise."

"Why'd you let him in the fucking car in the first place?" Danny asked as he leaned down and peered into Wiley's face long enough to confirm that Wiley wasn't home.

"Ben Franklin wen tell me do it," the driver said.

"And all the fucking Franklins I gave you didn't say anything?"

"Dey tol' me you no want no shit right outside da fuckin' show."

"You got that right," Danny said as he picked up the Glock. "I can't take this where I'm headed. You want it?"

"Sure," the driver said. Danny tossed him the Glock, then went through Wiley's pockets and came up with a wallet, a set of car keys, and several folded hundred-dollar bills.

"You might as well take these, too," Danny said, tossing the driver the keys. "Looks like he has a rental car back at the auditorium."

"What I gonna do wit' da kine?" the driver said as he snatched the keys out of the air, but Danny ignored the question.

"Can you believe I was worried about this stupid motherfucker?" Danny asked instead, but the driver just stood there with the car keys in one hand and the Glock in the other and gave no indication at all of whether he could believe Danny or not.

"Welcome home, Wiley," Danny said next, dropping it almost directly into Wiley's left ear. "Stupid as you are, you should fit in fine around here." Then he rose, picked up his leather satchel, and began to walk toward the nearest door.

"Hey!" the driver said. "What about dis moddafuckah?"

"Drop his sorry ass somewhere," Danny said over his shoulder as he walked. "Isn't that what you motherfucking do?"

FIFTY-EIGHT

The first thing I saw when I woke up was the WELCOME TO HILO sign. The limo's lights were off, but the letters in the sign were all painted white and gleamed enough in the glow from the nearest streetlight to be visible from where we were parked across the street.

The second thing I saw was the same as the first, because when I tried to move my head to look to my left I discovered I was almost buried in crushed ice from the neck up.

"No move your head, brah," the driver advised from my immediate left. "Gonna t'row ice everywheah, you move."

"Isn't that the sign on the way out of the airport?" I asked.

"Yeah," the driver said.

"Why'd you stop here?"

"Wanna welcome you to Hilo, dat's why."

"Thanks."

"You welcome, brah."

"How long was I out?"

"Two minutes, mebbe t'ree."

I reached up slowly and explored my head with my hands. I discovered one bag of ice propped against my left temple and another balanced precariously on top of my right eye. I was reclining slightly in the front passenger seat, so I held onto both bags of ice and tried to sit up straight.

Apparently the driver was on to what I was doing, because when I moved, my seat moved right with me. I could look around now that I was holding on to the ice, so I turned stiffly in his direction.

"You've got a deft touch," I said, thinking back to the last person who had hit me upside the head with just the right amount of force.

"T'anks," the driver said, grinning slightly. He was turned toward me with his back partially propped against the door, his eyes focused on me, and his hands wrapped around the Glock and a phone.

"I used to know another guy with a touch like that," I said, "but he's dead now."

"Everybody dies, yeah?" he said with a shrug.

I was tempted to shrug back, but my head hurt like hell whenever I moved. On the positive side, I was feeling no dizziness or nausea. I was beginning to go numb where the bags were touching my skin, but I had no complaints about that.

"Where'd you get the ice?" I asked.

"Top of da line, dis ride," he said. "Got da kine in da bah."

"So what's next? Cocktails?"

"Up to you, brah."

"If it were up to me, Dannyboy would be back in the car."

"Can, you know."

"How? You just dropped him at his plane."

"Gimme a t'ousand, I pick da fuckah back up again."

"A thousand?"

"Cost me to hold da bird, dat's why," he said, and he brandished the phone in his left hand while he said it. "No gonna take off till I call."

"Two or three minutes ago, I would have sworn you were working for Danny."

"Dat job is *pau*, brah."

"*Pau?*" I asked.

"Ovah. Lookin' fo' a new job now."

"It wasn't over when you let me in the car in the first place."

"I know he no want no hassle on da way out," he said.

"How'd you know I'd go for this?"

"You heah, brah. Gave me a hundred just to wait in da cah."

"What the fuck is your name?" I asked.

"Santiago," he said.

"My name is Wiley," I said, and I extended my right hand in his direction. I had to drop the ice in that hand to do it, and he had to drop the Glock to reciprocate, but we both did what had to be done and shook hands.

"Pleased to meet you," I said.

"Likewise," he said.

"You're on, Santiago," I said, but when I dropped the ice in my left hand and went in my pocket for the thousand, I discovered a financial shortfall I hadn't noticed earlier.

"No problem," Santiago said as he watched me fumble through my pockets. "We get 'em back when we pick up da moddafuckah, yeah?"

"Yeah," I said.

"Heah," he said, and he handed me the Glock and the keys to the rental car. I took both of the items without another word, and then I sat back in that same silence and watched as he nudged the limo to life and pointed it back in Dannyboy's direction.

As soon as we were rolling toward the terminal, Santiago spoke into the phone in his hand. "We on, brah," he said. "Drop da moddafuckah." Then he slipped the phone into the pocket on the front of his shirt and drove.

FIFTY-NINE

Danny took one look at the chopper waiting in front of him and almost turned around on the spot. *That stupid bitch,* he said to himself. *I was thinking a small jet—or a fucking plane, at the very least.* But it didn't take him long to remember that the direction from which he had come was no longer available to him, and the impulse to turn around dissipated quickly.

"Let me guess," Danny said when he reached the gray-haired Hawaiian waiting for him at the helicopter's door. "You flew in Nam, right?"

"That's right," the Hawaiian said flatly.

Mister Personality, Danny thought. *Just what I need tonight.* "Please don't tell me we're going to Honolulu in this thing," he said.

"Maui," he said. "She has you going commercial from there."

"How long will that take?" Danny said, but what he was thinking was this: *Not that bad an option, really, all things considered.*

"That depends a lot on the wind, actually. But it's not long—Maui is right next door."

I know where Maui is, Danny thought. *You can skip the geography lesson.* "Let's do this, then," he said.

"It will be a minute or two," the pilot said. "I don't have clearance to leave yet."

"Whatever," Danny said. He tossed his satchel onto the floor of the chopper and leaned against the side. He watched the pilot idly while his mind raced ahead to consideration of the task in front of him.

I'll have to be light on my feet to make this work, he said to himself, *but how much of a problem is that? Dannyboy is nothing if not light on his feet.*

He began to mull over the specifics of setting up in Singapore for a while, but as the minutes began to stack up his observation of the pilot steadily became more intrusive. He tried to visualize the thick brown man with big shoulders and muscular arms three decades earlier, a Hawaiian cowboy astride an Army Huey as he rodeoed from one end of Vietnam to the other.

"Were there many Hawaiian helicopter pilots over there?" Danny asked.

"No," the pilot said. "Why?"

I didn't think so, Danny thought. "You're the first one I've met," he said.

"How big is your sample?"

"You talk kind of funny for a local boy."

"A lot of us speak English," he said.

"I think you know what I mean," Danny said. He looked at the pilot sharply for a moment, then turned inward again. *And my sample is bigger than you might imagine,* Danny thought. *When your father dies in Vietnam before you are born, you tend to study the conflict there rather closely later in life.*

Danny was still lost in his own thoughts when the pilot went into his pocket for a phone. After a brief moment with the phone pressed to his ear, he returned it to his pocket and looked at Danny like the bearer of bad news.

"What's up?" Danny asked.

"Your flight's been canceled," the pilot said, and he hooked Danny so hard under his rib cage that Danny believed air had been abolished. Danny dropped to the ground as if he had been leaning on the air that was no longer in existence, and he writhed there helplessly while he struggled to breathe.

The struggle eventually paid off, but the next wave of bad news washed over Danny as soon as he got his lungs working again: The first thing he saw when he looked up was the approach of Wiley and the limo driver.

Geez, Danny thought as a sharp vision of his mother saying the exact same word flashed across his mind. *What did I ever do to deserve this shit?*

SIXTY

By the time we got to him, Danny was bent over the ground on his hands and knees like he was drawing a breath for the very first time. Santiago grabbed him by one arm and the chopper pilot grabbed the other while I leaned into the helicopter and retrieved Danny's satchel. A moment later, everyone but the pilot was rolling out of the parking lot in Santiago's limo.

The car turned right, and the WELCOME TO HILO sign whisked by in three or four blinks of an eye. When he reached Highway 11, Santiago turned toward the ocean, but he immediately turned right again and parked us in a secluded grassy area shielded by trees on three sides and one end of the airport complex on the fourth.

The sky opened as soon as we stopped, and no one spoke while a day's worth of water poured down on us in two or three minutes. I watched it fall through the window to my left, and the first thing that flashed across my mind was the utter frivolity of all the complaints about rain back in Portland.

"Now what?" Danny asked, which brought my mind back to matters closer at hand. He was crumpled in the corner of the seat across from me, but I took the fact that he was able to speak as evidence that he had recovered from his abbreviated charter flight.

"I don't know, Danny," I said. "I really don't."

"Look," he said, "I could have killed you earlier, but I didn't. I just want to point that out."

"I noticed that, Danny."

"That should count for something."

"You did what you did because it was better for you, just like everything else you do. But I'm still counting it."

"I don't know why you don't just let me go," he said. "You're not a cold-blooded killer, and I'm not going back to Portland with you."

"That is the quandary exactly," I said. "You have a good eye for the essential, Danny."

"It sounds like you know I'm right."

"As far as you went."

"What?"

"I think you may have overlooked an option or two."

"Like what?"

"Like waiting here until Leon feels up to a trip to paradise."

"Why would I want to do that?"

"I didn't say you'd want to."

"When you think about it, why don't I just open the door and walk away?"

"Because you're likely to drown if you do."

"I know how to swim."

"If you think that'll work for you," I said, "go ahead and do it."

Danny did nothing for the next few heartbeats, except to sit up a little straighter and stare at me more intently.

"How long have we been playing in the same poker games?" he asked as soon as he got tired of keeping his mouth shut.

"I don't know," I said. "Quite a while."

"However long it's been, I've never been able to figure out what you're holding."

"You know *exactly* what I'm holding now," I said, and I wiggled the Glock in my left hand a little to remind him.

"You know what I mean," he said. "Would you really shoot me?"

"I can shoot you without trying to kill you. Just because I can't blow your brains out the way Leon would doesn't mean I can't blow off a foot or something."

"Why'd you say foot?" Danny asked. "Was all that talk a couple of years ago about you shooting Sylvester and his bodyguard in the foot actually true?"

"Similar situation, actually. I shot them in the foot, then Leon came around and shot 'em the rest of the way off the planet."

"That was totally different, though. That was in the heat of the moment, right? This is cold, Wiley. This is too cold for you."

"You'll start to bleed if you step out of this car, Danny. If you were paying attention at all since you've known me, you'd know that."

"Why?" he asked. "I haven't done anything to you!"

"You seem to think if you say something often enough, you can make it be true."

"What I'm saying *is* true! *Lester's* the guy you should be talking to."

"You killed the kid, Danny, and you caused Julie's rape even if you didn't rip off a piece of her yourself. I'm going to put a hole in you somewhere if you walk out of this car."

"Even if you believe what you just said about me," he said as he opened the door closest to him, "you're not going to shoot me. You're bluffing, Wiley."

"Santiago," I said, and Danny froze when I said it. "Do you have a first-aid kit in this thing?"

"Top of da line ride, brah," he said. "You know I got da kine."

"Cute," Danny said, "but it doesn't change a thing. You're not Leon, and you never will be." Then he stepped out of the car and began walking toward the highway behind us.

I went out through the same door. The rain had stopped, but it had been so heavy that the air still felt wet. I watched Danny as he moved away, and when he was three or four feet beyond the end of the limo, I pointed the Glock in his direction and pulled the trigger.

SIXTY-ONE

Danny dropped like a dead duck when the bullet winged his left leg, but unlike a duck, he couldn't float on the small lake the rain had created on the road to the highway. He sprawled face first in the water and tried without much success to turn his lungs into gills until Wiley rolled him over.

The back of Danny's head was still in water up to his earlobes in his new position, but air was suddenly a lot more accessible. He lay there and breathed it in and out while Wiley tried to assess his condition.

"Is the gun going off here gonna cause us a problem?" Wiley asked. *Why in hell are you asking me?* Danny thought, but he realized where the question had been directed when Santiago's voice dropped on him from behind Wiley somewhere.

"Not," Santiago said. "Sound no carry in da wet like dis."

Good, Danny thought. *Even the victim doesn't want the police rolling up on us right now.*

"Get up," Wiley said, and it took a moment or two of silence before Danny realized the words were meant for him this time.

"Get up?" he said. "You just shot me in the leg!"

"You can stand on one leg," Wiley said, and he reached down with the hand that wasn't holding the Glock. Danny reached up, grabbed Wiley's hand with both of his own, and rose until he was standing on his right leg with one arm around Wiley's shoulder. He could feel water from the impromptu lake running in warm rivulets under his clothes, juxtaposed oddly with the searing fire radiating from his left calf.

Wiley pivoted as soon as Danny seemed to be semiambulatory and began to lead him back to the limo. Danny watched Santiago pull a first-aid kit and a sheet of clear plastic out of the trunk as they approached.

One seat in the limo was swathed in the plastic by the time Danny limped back to the car, leaning on Wiley's free arm every step of the way. Wiley eased him through the door, and the first thing Danny heard as he stretched out with his left leg propped on the plastic was the snick of a switchblade knife.

Danny knew in his head that it made no sense to haul him into the limo just to kill him with a knife, but his sphincter tightened up at the sound like it had a mind of its own. He felt his eyes getting bigger as he looked around, but what he saw was Santiago slicing the leg of his slacks away from the wound on his calf.

"You barely hit 'em, brah," Santiago said as he fumbled with his first-aid kit.

"That's what I was tryin' to do," Wiley said from just outside the limo door.

"Dis no hurt da kine," Santiago said, holding up a bottle of hydrogen peroxide where Danny could see it. Then he opened the bottle and began to pour some of the liquid inside directly on the gash on Danny's leg.

"Shit!" Danny shouted. "The fuck that doesn't hurt!"

"I go wit' da mert'iolate instead," Santiago said, "you gonna t'ink dis mo' bettah da kine, I promise." He mopped up the runoff of peroxide with a handful of gauze, then adroitly tied a dressing where it would do the most good.

"You've done this before," Wiley said from his vantage point off Santiago's shoulder.

"Mebbe now and den," he said as he repacked the kit. "Where you wanna go now, brah?"

"Do you have a suggestion?"

"Can find someone to do dis guy, you know."

"Really?"

"Somebody do 'em fo' ice, I t'ink."

"Ice?"

"Crystal met'. Fuckin' shit killin' us, brah."

Wiley didn't respond to that, so Danny stood there unsteadily and watched the words already spoken float above his head like mosquitoes circling for supper.

"Wiley, come on," he said when he couldn't stand the silence any longer. "You're thinking about contracting me out to some methamphetamine freak?"

Wiley shook his head—reluctantly, it seemed to Danny. "He's right," Wiley said finally. "I can't go there."

"No t'ink so," Santiago said. "Mebbe you need mo' time, yeah?"

"Maybe," Wiley said, and Danny perked up substantially at this new direction in the conversation. *Now you're talking,* he said to himself. *Nothing suits me better right now than a little more time.*

"Got da kine place you can stay," Santiago said. "A hundred a day, as many days as you want."

"I can stay at a hotel for that," Wiley said.

"Hotel give you stink-eye fo' dis one," Santiago said with a nod in Danny's direction. "Plus I help you keep one eye on him fo' free, yeah?"

"Plus it's his money anyway, right?"

And worth every dime, Danny said without a sound.

"Now you talkin', brah."

"You're on," Wiley said. He slipped around Santiago and

into the seat opposite Danny, and Santiago stepped out with his first-aid kit and closed the door. All three of them settled into silence again, but Danny was virtually shouting into his inner ear.

Praise the Lord and pass the plate, Danny said to himself, and then he settled into the plastic sheet on his seat and began to wait.

SIXTY-TWO

My head began to throb as soon as I leaned into the cushions of my seat, but somehow I felt more comfortable with
the pain than with the adrenaline rush that had pushed it
aside while I was dealing with Danny's attempt to depart.
There seemed to be a loose connection between the sharp
pulsations inside my head and the beating of my heart, and
I almost savored the way it reminded me that pain afflicts
only the living.

Santiago wheeled the limo around and plowed through
Danny's lake. He turned right when we reached the highway, and he did the same thing at the light in front of a
twenty-four-hour pancake house a moment later.

I watched through the window next to me as we rambled
by Hilo's port facilities. What I could see in the dripping darkness of the night resonated with the same degree of tropical al-
lure I might have experienced in Gary, Indiana, or Newark,
New Jersey, only on a much smaller scale. I was wondering
what had happened to the signposts of paradise when we
passed a bright collection of lights stacked ten or fifteen stories
high on the water.

"Fuckin' cruise ship," Santiago said as though he could read
the question in my mind. "T'ousands of tourists every fuckin'
week."

"I would have thought a limo driver would be gung-ho for the tourist industry," I said.

"Fuck 'em," he said.

I turned away from the window while I processed that comment and looked at Dannyboy instead. He was stretched out on his plastic-covered seat with his eyes closed, but his body looked about as relaxed as my throbbing head felt.

"Don't even think about it, Danny," I said.

"Now you're trying to control what I think?" he asked. "You'll find that's a bit harder than controlling when I come and go."

I couldn't think of a way to contradict that, so I turned back to the window without a response. I continued to eye the drab metallic buildings through the thin veil of pain inside my head.

It wasn't long before Santiago pulled the plug on me. He drove off to the side of the road when we reached a narrow beachside park jammed with makeshift tents. He climbed out of the car and opened the door next to me.

"Let's go," I said, and Danny went. I followed behind him until all three of us were standing next to the limo as a steady stream of traffic flowed by us in both directions.

"Where's everyone goin'?" I asked.

"Nowheah," Santiago said, and the word floated on the dense air between us until he stepped into a gap in the traffic and began to cross the road. I followed him, and Danny followed me, if that word describes moving in tandem with someone holding a Glock in one hand and your shoulder with the other. I kept the Glock pressed against my leg in hopes that it wouldn't be obvious to everyone we passed, but I knew Danny was vividly aware of it.

Lanterns lit most of the tents, and small groups of brown people were congregated in each of them. I heard snatches of pidgin and music as we moved across the wet, spongy ground between the tents, but Santiago spoke to no one, and no one spoke to him. He finally stopped at a dark tent on the edge of the encampment, and we stopped with him.

"*Tutu,*" he said softly into the darkness, and then he waited. Danny and I waited, too, and I used the time to watch the full moon play hide-and-seek with the rain clouds scurrying across the night sky.

After a moment or two, a shadow moved in the darkness and slowly emerged from the tent. The intermittent moonlight eventually revealed a wide, thick brown woman with long, luminous silver hair that caught the flickering light and tossed it back whenever the woman moved.

The woman somehow projected the weight of advanced age around her, but the moonlight did nothing to confirm it. In that uncertain glow, her soft face seemed ageless, her massive body formless, nothing really rooted in a specific time and place except her deep brown eyes.

I don't know how long we stood there without another word, but I used all of it to look into those eyes whenever the light allowed, and she stood in front of me and used the same light in exactly the same way.

"Dey need stay heah fo' now," Santiago finally said, and the woman nodded and stepped away from the opening of the tent. I stepped aside, too, and Danny limped past us and under the tarp.

"Use the cot," Santiago said when Danny seemed to hesitate, so Danny slowly stretched out on an empty cot off to our left.

"Wiley," Santiago said then, "dis my *tutu* Grace." The woman stepped in my direction when he said that and pressed her warm cheek against mine, so I pressed back. Then she stepped away and moved to a lawn chair pointed at the ocean.

"*Tutu?*" I asked quietly.

"Grandmama," Santiago said.

"She looks more like me than you," I said.

"I got one Filipino side, too, dat's why."

"What is this place?" I asked.

"You got Hawaiian homelands across da street," he said. "Some of dem like to camp out ovah heah in da summah."

"What's next?" I asked.

"You watch 'em til I get back, den I do it."

I nodded, and he started to walk away. But after two or three steps, he turned around and came back. "One t'ing, brah," he said. "*Tutu* don' talk da kine."

"No English?" I asked, thinking back to the words he had spoken to her earlier.

"Nah," he said. "She no kine talk."

"What happened?"

"Not'ing," he said. "I t'ink she gonna talk soon as somet'ing do happen." Then he turned away again, and I watched him retrace our steps through the neighboring tents as the moon continued to play with the clouds.

SIXTY-THREE

Danny opened his eyes on a wet gray morning and was immediately punished for it. The first thing he saw was Wiley lounging in a canvas chair a foot or two from Danny's cot, the Glock resting on Wiley's leg like the postscript on a letter Danny hoped never to receive.

"What?" Danny said. "You thought I might walk in my sleep?"

"That's one of the problems with these things," Wiley said quietly, moving his eyes from Danny to the Glock and back again. "Once you have one, what do you do with it?"

I think I'd know what to do with it, Danny thought, but what he said was this: "So what's the plan? We sit here until one of us dies of natural causes?"

"Sounds kinda slow, doesn't it?" Wiley said.

"Sometimes slow is good, though," Danny said.

"True," Wiley said. "But I don't think this is one of those times."

"Sure it is. The one thing we don't want to do is rush into something we'll later regret."

"We?"

"Don't try to pretend we're not in this together, Wiley. We're joined at the hip on this thing."

Wiley apparently had no argument with that, because he rose from his chair without another word and stepped outside the tent. Danny followed his example, and a moment later they were both standing on a small patch of sand at the edge of the ocean.

The sky was the same color as the Glock in Wiley's hand, and so was the water. Danny found it difficult to determine where one stopped and the other started when his gaze drifted toward the horizon, but after he grew weary of grappling with that distinction he found something else to look at.

It began as a dark dot in the gray distance, bobbing gently with the undulation of the water. Eventually, the dot grew into a swimmer moving almost effortlessly toward the shore, and then the anonymous swimmer emerged from the water in front of them as a tall brown woman in a bright blue bikini top and blue surfer shorts.

Geez!! he thought. *I woke up in paradise this morning in spite of myself.*

The woman's body moved behind the bikini top like the material wasn't there, and Danny stood dumbly as she approached and tried to figure out exactly how that effect was achieved. He had no answer by the time she stopped three or four yards from where he and Wiley were standing and leaned forward until her long black hair streamed down in front of her.

Danny watched her wring the water out of her hair, then straighten up and toss the hair over her shoulder. Her brown breasts swayed beneath the skimpy blue material when she did that, and Danny savored the sight as though he had never seen a woman before.

Maybe I haven't, he thought. *Maybe this is the very first one.* At the very end of that thought, Danny got his first glimpse of the scar on the left side of the woman's face. She shook her head slightly in the process of readjusting her hair, and the scar screamed out at him—a mean, bitter streak of pale skin running erratically from the woman's left ear almost to the point of her chin.

"You should see the other guy," the woman said, which was when Danny realized the woman had been watching him study her. Then she walked around them without another word, and Danny turned unabashedly and watched her do it.

When she reached the tent, she picked up a large towel and put it to work. Danny also watched every moment of that process, and then he watched her discard the towel and slip into a loose shirt that almost shielded her lush body from his hot gaze.

Almost, Danny thought, *but not quite*. "Did you see that?" he said aloud, even though he already knew the answer to the question.

Wiley did not reply. His eyes were stuck on the woman, too, but he was transfixed as though he were staring at a ghost of the woman rather than the woman herself. The woman seemed to think this was funny, because she broke into a smile after a moment or two.

"I'm not quite finished with it yet," the woman said. Danny made no response to that because he had no clue what an appropriate response might be, but Wiley was apparently not similarly encumbered.

"No problem," Wiley said, a smile of his own finally cracking through the shocked expression on his face. "I can wait a little longer." Then he turned back toward the water, and before long his eyes were locked so far into the murky intersection of sky and ocean that Danny began to wonder if Wiley had somehow escaped his body and was no longer standing next to him.

"Earth to Wiley," Danny said. "What the fuck was that all about?"

"Do you believe in God, Danny?" Wiley asked, his eyes still gone but the voice coming from the space right next to Danny on the small patch of sand.

"What?"

"Do you believe in some kind of a higher being out there somewhere?"

Danny turned to look where Wiley's eyes were pointed, but he still couldn't see where the sky ended and the ocean began. "No," he said. "I don't think there is anything out there but water."

"That's what I used to think," Wiley said softly. "But we were wrong, Danny. Everything that ever was or ever will be is out there waiting for us."

"Great," Danny said. "My fate is in the hands of a lunatic."

"Not really," Wiley said as he turned toward the tent. "Your fate is in your own hands, Danny. It always has been."

"If that's the case, why don't you let me hold the gun for a while?"

"That would put *my* fate in your hands, too. The way that looks so far, I'm not too keen on joining you."

"Like I said, we're already joined at the hip in this."

"I admit that I'm stuck to you at the moment," Wiley said. "But you may be overstating the connection."

"I don't think so, Wiley. You're not stuck *to* me, you're stuck *with* me. And you don't have the balls to do anything about it."

"Right as the Hilo rain, Dannyboy," Wiley said, his voice almost too quiet to hear as he started a slow stroll toward the tent and the scarred woman waiting there for them.

Danny heard every word, quiet or not, and he liked the

way they sounded. But Danny was chilled to the core by the next words he heard, which were these:

"That's why I'm thinking about letting God take care of us," Wiley said, and he looked dead serious when he said it.

SIXTY-FOUR

I couldn't get either the woman or the ocean out of my head. We have the same ocean washing up against the western edge of Oregon, of course, but somehow it had never hit me the same way there as it did that morning on the eastern edge of the Big Island.

We have women in Oregon, too—even a few I would die for without a second thought—but I didn't have a first thought in my head about any of them while this woman was in front of me.

Danny, however, seemed to have something a little less profound on his mind. "What *did* happen to the other guy?" he asked when we got back to the tent.

The woman looked up at him peacefully from the lounge chair Grandmama Grace had used the night before, and I could almost see the wheels turning in her mind while she considered whether or not to respond to the question.

"He died," she said when her deliberation was done. "I slit his throat with the same knife he used on me."

"Is that really what happened?"

"You have no way of evaluating that, do you?" she said. "That makes your question somewhat pointless, doesn't it?"

"Not really," Danny said. "Even bald-faced lies can tell you quite a bit about the person you're talking to."

"Only if you can distinguish the lies from the truth."

"Whatever," Danny said. "Go ahead and finish the story."

"He cut me, I cut him, he died. End of story."

"Someone strong enough to slash your face like that in the first place, how'd you get the knife away from him?"

"He eventually fell asleep," the woman said.

"Wow," Danny said. "Makes you sound like a dangerous person."

"Don't you think everyone is dangerous," she asked, "given the right set of circumstances?"

"I suppose so," Danny said. He turned to look at me for a moment or two, and I imagined him calculating whether our present circumstances were the right set to make a dangerous person out of me. When the moment or two had passed, he returned his gaze to the woman.

"You look like you're from here," he said, "but you don't sound like it."

"We can make a lot of sounds over here," she said. "Just like real people."

"That's not what I meant."

"Really?"

"Really."

"How odd that you didn't say what you actually meant, then."

"Are you this prickly with everyone," Danny asked, shaking his head slowly, "or is it just me?"

"Did you think I was 'prickly' while you were watching me come out of the water?"

"No."

"I was exactly the same person then that I am now," she said softly as she pushed her hair back from her face with both hands. "Perhaps your ability to perceive people needs a little work."

"Perhaps," Danny said. "I'd love an opportunity to perceive *you* a little better."

"I get that a lot. Especially if I keep my face turned just right." Then she turned her face just wrong, and I took another good look at the scar and the woman who went with it. She turned her eyes from Danny to me while I did it, and she kept them there when Danny spoke again.

"Up until right now," he said, "I would have deserved that crack. In your case, I don't. I guess I've never met anyone like you before."

"There *isn't* anyone like me," she said as she rose effortlessly from the lounge chair, still looking at me rather than Danny. "But there isn't anyone like any of the other people you have met, either."

"I see what you're saying," Danny said.

She let those words drift off somewhere, and after an awkward silence she stepped up and wrapped her arms around my shoulders. "Welcome home," she said, her lips brushing softly against my cheek as she said it.

"Thank you," I said.

"You can trust the ocean," she said. "I think you'll be fine."

I stood there dumbly for a moment, savoring the comfort of her strong brown arms. I wanted to return her embrace, but I was still holding the Glock in my left hand. I finally wrapped my right arm around her and hugged her back as hard as I could.

"What's up with this?" Danny said. "I do all the work, and he gets all the hugs."

"I can't reach across the gap between us," she said as she broke away from me and turned her attention back to Danny. "But I pray the gods treat you fairly once you're out there."

"Out where?" Danny asked, but the woman walked away from both of us. I watched her pick her way between the neighboring tents, and so did Danny.

"Who was that?" Danny asked. "And what the fuck was that about?"

"I don't know, actually," I said.

"You were talking like you knew each other."

"We've met, but I don't know her," I said as I looked beyond the woman and saw what had triggered her departure. Santiago and a pair of men I didn't know were slowly making their way toward us with a two-man kayak on their shoulders, and beyond them I could see Grandmama Grace even more slowly following in their footsteps.

"The answer to your second question approaches even as we speak," I said.

"What?" Danny said, tracing the direction of my eyes with his own. "The fucking kayak?"

"Precisely," I said. "You and I are about to go on our very own sea cruise, Danny."

SIXTY-FIVE

The kayak cut through the gentle swell like an arrow as the paddlers found a rhythm together, but Danny wouldn't have picked a direction that drew them away from the shore so rapidly.

"Now you've really flipped your fucking lid," Danny said.

"I don't mind if you talk as long as you keep paddling," Wiley said from the seat behind Danny, and Danny started stroking the gray water with the wooden paddle again. The collection of tents on the beach was behind them somewhere, and Danny could feel them receding as he stared into the empty ocean in front of him.

They both bent into the task of paddling, and the kayak sliced its way through the gray of the sky and the gray of the water simultaneously. After fifteen or twenty minutes of effort, they were engulfed in a squall so close upon them that Danny could see nothing but gray no matter which direction he looked.

"So what are you hoping to achieve by this?" Danny asked. "I'll have a heart attack, maybe?"

"That would work for me," Wiley said.

"I wouldn't count on that," Danny said.

"I'm not."

"What, then?"

"I'm hoping you'll experience an epiphany, Danny, to tell you the truth. I'm hoping the gods will open your eyes to the wisdom of going back to Portland with me if we get out here far enough."

Then we can stop right now, you fucking lunatic, Danny thought. *My eyes are already open, and I am really beginning to like what I see.*

"An epiphany?" Danny asked.

"Exactly," Wiley said.

"Doesn't that require the existence of a divine being of some sort?"

"Yes."

"Then you're screwed, Wiley. I told you earlier there's nothing out here but water."

"Yes, you did. I think you're wrong."

"Believe me, if that gun didn't bring an epiphany on, nothing will."

"Maybe that's the problem," Wiley said. "Maybe the gun's in the way."

Absolutely, Danny said to himself. *There's a thought I hope you follow to its logical conclusion.* Then something gray glinted off to his right and plunked into the water, and Danny felt his heart rise in his chest like it had suddenly sprouted wings.

"Are you kidding me?" he asked.

"No," Wiley said.

"Did you just dump the gun?"

"Yes."

"Why would you do that? What's the catch?"

"There's no catch, Danny. It's just you, me, and the gods out here now."

"No," Danny said. "It's just you and me." He stopped paddling and started to run escape scenarios through his head, but he had yet to work past the problem of being stuck in the seat right in front of Wiley. Within seconds he felt the water rushing into the seat well around him.

"Hey!" he said sharply.

"This isn't a round-trip ride," Wiley said. "We'll have to find another way back."

"You really are nuts!" Danny shouted. "I can't believe we've been letting you walk around loose all these years!" He wanted to say more, but the rapid transformation of their craft from kayak to submarine began to demand Danny's attention. He focused for a moment on kicking his feet free of the seat well and launching himself into the water, and he could feel Wiley doing something similar behind him.

Danny swallowed more seawater than he wanted in the process of getting his arms and legs coordinated, but he was treading water comfortably in a moment or two. He could see Wiley doing the same thing four or five yards away, and they watched each other silently until Danny couldn't stand it any longer.

"What was this supposed to accomplish?" Danny asked. "Even if we make it back to the beach, what will have changed?"

Wiley's head dipped below the surface, and Danny lost track of him for a while. Then Wiley's head bobbed up again in a new location, still about the same distance from Danny but a few yards to the right.

"Everything has changed already," Wiley said finally. "You're free to do whatever you want from this point on."

"I still don't get it," Danny said. "Why are you doing this?"

Wiley disappeared again and bobbed up a few more yards to Danny's right. "What I was doing before wasn't working," Wiley said.

"And you think this will?"

"Probably," Wiley said before he dipped below the surface just to rise again even more to the right.

"You really believe this epiphany crap?"

"I didn't say I believed it, Danny. I said I was hoping for it."

"Then tell me what you do believe."

Wiley ducked that question momentarily, resurfacing in the opposite direction this time. "I believe you'll try to bury me at sea," he said.

"Why would you want that?" Danny said, but what he thought was this: *The idiot got that one right, didn't he?*

This time when Wiley disappeared, he stayed gone long enough to make Danny uneasy. It seemed to Danny that the gray swells began to grow as he waited, and he was looking around on the outer edges of panic when Wiley resurfaced directly behind him.

"Because I think self-defense is the only way I can actually kill you, Danny."

"You could be the one who gets killed, though," Danny said.

"True," Wiley said. "That's where the gods come in."

I see, Danny said to himself as Wiley pulled his disappearing act one more time. *But since there are no fucking gods, you beautiful fucking idiot, I have to think I'll like where that leaves us better than you will.*

SIXTY-SIX

I had a pair of aces in the hole when I hit the water with Danny, but I had played enough hands of Hold'em to know that aces don't always hold up. You make the moves you want to make and then hope for the best, and that's exactly what I did in the ocean that day.

My first move was to keep Danny talking as long as I could. This brought my first ace into play, because it soon became obvious that only one of us knew the difference between bobbing and treading water. I was able to rest every time my head dipped below the surface, while Danny kept right on pumping those comely arms and legs of his to keep his pretty head out of the water.

Danny made the next move when he finally got tired of talking, but that only served to draw my second ace into action. I knew in advance exactly what that move was going to be, and I had put four or five yards between us to absorb it. When he came at me, my response was modulated flight: I swam away when he swam toward me, and I stopped to rest when he stopped. Except that I bobbed then and he continued to tread water, which brought us right back where we started—me resting a lot more than he did.

I don't know how often we repeated this cycle, but I do know he only laid a hand on me once. He grabbed my left ankle and pulled, but his grip slipped enough for me to break away when I kicked him in the face with my other foot.

He might have learned to bob that time, because he went under from the force of the blow. He came up flailing his limbs and spitting water, though, so I knew my aces were still the top cards in play.

"You son of a bitch!" he sputtered, his chest heaving as he tried to calm himself. My only response to that was to drop out of sight, this time down two or three body lengths as he lunged toward me again. I stroked underwater toward his previous location, and when I resurfaced we had basically switched places.

Danny was looking off in the wrong direction—a little frantically, it seemed to me—so I tried to point out an alternative course of action.

"You don't have to do this, Danny," I said. He spun in the water to face me, and one look at his face convinced me I was wrong—he did have to do exactly what he was trying to do. He came at me again, and I swam away, and we continued that cycle for many minutes more.

I had seen Danny sink the same way in many a Hold'em game, him with the weaker cards but waiting for a miracle from the dealer. Sometimes the dealer came through, but usually he did not, a distinction that is utterly random in the short term but completely preordained in the long.

Danny eventually drained off his last drop of adrenaline. His sudden surges became less frequent and packed less punch, and he began to sag lower in the water while trying to recover. I watched him from the far side of the gap between us as a more accurate appreciation of his perilous situation slowly replaced the vanishing adrenaline.

That's when he began to plead, to weep, to rant, to curse. Some of what he said I heard, some I did not. I continued to bob, down one place and up in another.

"Help me!"

"I don't deserve—"

"Fuck you, you fucking faggot!"

"What did I ever do—"

"—last much longer, Wiley!"

The longer these words rolled out of his mouth, the weaker he became. I made the same response to each word: I bobbed relentlessly, up and down one way, up and down another way, some of his words skipping off the water over my head and some of them hitting home.

I don't think Danny drowned that day. I think he died right before my eyes, the life leaking out of his mouth as he spoke. When all of it was gone, he sank beneath the surface and I never saw him again.

SIXTY-SEVEN

I was alone with the gods after Danny was gone, and they spared me for a while. I have no idea why; some are spared and some are not, the gods in Hawai'i apparently being every bit as capricious as their cousins in Greece or Rome.

The first sign of my favored status appeared as rain, a torrential downpour so thick I could drink rainwater right out of the sky. When my thirst was slaked, the sun knifed through the clouds and increased the visibility around me both coming and going. The color of the water around me changed from gray to blue with the change in the sky as I continued to bob my way through the morning.

I felt totally at home in the ocean, at peace, serene. I didn't understand it. It made no logical sense; there was no precedent for it and no premonition of it anywhere in my life. Still, there I was, confident that I could ride the gentle swells around me for the rest of my life.

I thought from time to time about beginning the long swim to the shore, but I spit the thought out like seawater as soon as I remembered that I had no idea which direction that might be. Then I would bob some more, resting regularly, until the thought came back again.

I thought of other things, too. Was I more or less guilty because I had been unable to take Danny's life, yet had watched him slowly lose it without blinking an eye? How would that be tabulated when the final calculations were made?

And how far away could that final reckoning possibly be? Certainly not days—could anyone bob in the Pacific for days, even here where the water ran warm? Hours, then? Or was it down to minutes yet?

Beyond those thoughts, visions of people living and dead flashed through my mind, one kind jumbled together with the other as though the distinction between the two had sunk in the sea with Danny. Who would miss me, who would welcome me from the other side?

What to make of Leon, I wondered, the rock who anchored all of us now slowly crumbling in a hospital room? Or Ronetta and Julie, who loved me in their separate ways but hated the life that had evolved around me? Or Alix, who had made a career out of doing something primal with men that she could not for the life of her draw out of me? Or Miriam and Elmer, who died too soon? Or Dookie and Fernando, who died too late? Or most of all, sweet Lizzie, the daughter who never should have died at all?

I shuddered when these thoughts led me to the coldest of realizations—that I would keenly miss no one, that the dead called me more profoundly than anyone among the living, that I would rather seek a new beginning with the daughter who died than pursue the pale connections I had formed among her many survivors.

Then a vision of the woman with a scar on her face floated into my head, a vision that ran counter to my previous thinking in a way I didn't fully comprehend. I could hear her calling me from the side of life, but who was she, and what did she signify?

Eventually, the wind kicked up above me, and the water around me began to churn. The silence I had grown accustomed to also fell away, banished by the sound of a thousand seagull wings beating incessantly right outside my ears every time I surfaced. I watched the water whip into a whirlpool around me, and after a long ride on that watery edge I let go of myself and dropped into the blissful vortex like a stone.

Suddenly, a sea serpent appeared at my side. She wrapped her strong brown tentacles around me and folded me close to her warm body. I marveled at the sleek smoothness of her skin where the scales should have been, and rubbed my shriveled face against it until the water fell away from both of us and we rose in the windblown sky like birds.

SIXTY-EIGHT

I woke up naked on the cot where Danny had spent his last night, although it took me a while to recognize it. My first impression was only that I had passed from my previous realm to a new one, somewhere much drier and colder than the realm I had left behind.

Before I even opened my eyes, I discovered that I was buried up to my chin in blankets. They apparently were unable to keep my teeth from clacking uncontrollably against each other as I shivered, but I made a little progress toward that end by wrapping my arms around myself and rubbing vigorously.

I raised my head slowly as I was doing this, and the first thing I saw was the woman with a scar across one side of her face. She was rising from the lounge chair just outside the tent, the sun bathing her wounded face as she moved. She floated to a small gas grill a few steps to her right, lifted the lid from an aluminum pot, and poured a steaming liquid into a coffee mug resting on a wooden television tray. Then she put the pot back where she had found it, replaced the lid, walked the coffee mug to the side of the cot, and extended it in my direction.

I watched this sequence of movements as if entranced.

She was wearing a sleeveless pullover, and her biceps rippled under her brown skin every time her bare arms moved. Her wide shoulders were exquisitely muscled, too, but she moved with the unmistakable fluidity of someone who had built her body in the water rather than a weight room.

I sat up unsteadily and swung my bare feet to the ground. I took the mug in both hands and let the heat radiate through my fingers while I stared into the woman's deep brown eyes.

"Thank you," I said. "For everything."

"You're welcome," she said.

I leaned over the mug for a while and inhaled a warm fragrance faintly reminiscent of the sea I had recently left behind me. The warmth worked its way through my nostrils and fingers simultaneously, and when I finally tried a taste of the liquid the heat burned through my mouth and throat as well.

"That's hot," I said, shaking my head almost involuntarily.

"You need the heat," she said.

"How did I get here?" I asked as I tiptoed toward another sip from the mug.

"By helicopter," she said.

"So that's where you came from," I said. "I thought you were a sea serpent of some kind."

"I am," she said simply as she shifted to the back of the tent and picked up a thin quilt. Then she returned to my side, draped the quilt over my bare shoulders, and sat down on the cot next to me.

I could feel the touch of her body against mine as she found a seat on the cot, the space she had left between us somehow just an extension of our bodies—or maybe a contact zone in which her neurons and mine suddenly focused on rubbing against each other. I looked at her closely to determine whether she could feel it, too, but I didn't know her well enough to interpret the hint of a grin in the eyes that looked back at me.

I continued to carefully sip the broth, and it slowly chased the chill from my body. In four or five minutes, I was back to normal—if you didn't count the knot on the left side of my head or my swollen right eye, both souvenirs of that previous realm where Santiago and Danny had been on the same team and Danny had still been alive.

"Now can I ask you something?" she said after no one had spoken for a while.

"Sure," I said.

"How did you get the scars on your back?" she asked, and then she pressed her left hand on the quilt where it draped over my left shoulder. "And this one here," she added, her fingers perfectly positioned over the mark high above my heart that lined up with one of the scars on my back.

"From some bad men with guns," I said.

"What happened to them?" she asked.

"They all died."

"Does that bother you?"

"More and more," I said.

"I thought so," she said soberly, her hand moving from my shoulder to the wounded side of her face. "I feel that way sometimes, too."

"Even though they deserved it," I said.

"The thing is," she said, "we all deserve it."

"Exactly," I said.

She removed her hand from her face then and eased back into her own space, but somehow she took me with her as she did it. I could smell her every time I inhaled—the clean aroma of strong soap and the haunting scent of the sea layered on top of something subtly primal rooted firmly in the rocky earth beneath our feet. I sat there in another moment of silence, content to do nothing but breathe in and breathe out, and she sat next to me and watched me do it with the same grin still playing in her eyes.

"How did you find me out there?" I asked, more to break the silence than to learn the answer.

"You were right in the center of a sunbeam," she said. "It was like the gods had opened up a crease in the clouds and trained a spotlight on your head."

"Seriously," I said.

"I am serious. It was like a beacon—we flew right to you."

"Why are you helping me like this?"

"You hired Santiago," she said. "The rest of us kind of go with the package."

"I didn't hire him for all this," I said.

"I guess you need to work that out with him," she said.

"I'm starting to feel like I need to work something out with you."

"That won't be easy," she said, and the grin leaked away as if her eyes had suddenly been shot full of holes. "There are reasons why I'm not already with someone."

"It doesn't have to be easy," I said.

"Does that mean you're going to stay?"

"No."

"This thing isn't over yet, is it?"

"No."

"Is it going to end up killing you, after all?"

"It might," I said.

"And even if it doesn't, I suppose your situation there is complicated."

"Aren't they all?" I said.

"Mine isn't," she said, "but I am."

"Are we insane?" I asked.

"Probably," she said, the grin flooding back to its previous location.

"I suppose I should ask you one more question before I leave," I said.

"What's that?"

"What's your name?"

SIXTY-NINE

I watched Hilo drop away as the jet dipped toward Oahu, and no more than a moment later I was bouncing down the runway at Portland International. Somehow I changed planes in Honolulu and traversed the Pacific without registering a conscious thought, and somehow time stood still while I did it.

Fortunately, I had done some conscious thinking before I boarded the flight. I FedExed Danny's money to Leon, for one thing, mostly to avoid explaining all that cash if security happened to open the bag in the airport. I waited in Hilo until I could adequately navigate on land again, for another thing, which gave me an extra day of exposure to Georgiana.

"No kidding?" I asked when she told me that was her name. "I think one of my grandmothers had that name."

"So did one of mine," she said.

"Does that mean we're related?" I asked.

"Everyone is related," she said.

I replayed that conversation in my mind several times while I rolled with Junior from the airport to Emanuel, and Junior gave me plenty of space to do it. He stuck the Mercedes into the flow of the nighttime traffic, and all the way in on I-84 he kept his mouth shut and drove.

"How is he?" I asked finally.

"Good," Junior said, but it took him a lot longer to say it than I thought it should have.

"What?" I asked.

"You'll see," he said, and after five more minutes of silence he drove up to the front door of the hospital and proved himself right.

Leon was coming out the door in a wheelchair as we rolled to a stop. A heavyset nurse with a scowl wrapped around her face two or three times was pushing the chair, and she looked angry enough to make me question what her ultimate destination might be.

"If you can't walk out," I said as I climbed out of the car, "should you be leavin'?"

"The ride was her idea, not mine," Leon said as he rose from the chair. "I didn't feel like fightin' her for the right to walk."

"You knew you couldn't win, is all it was," the nurse said.

"Please," Leon said, winking at me.

"Don't you *please* me," the nurse said. "You couldn't whup me on the best day of your life, Leon, and that sure as hell ain't today."

"Is he leavin' too soon?" I asked.

"Only a week or two," she said.

"Go find someone sick to nurse," Leon said as he climbed into the seat next to Junior that I had vacated. "And thanks, sweetheart. Seriously."

"Keep him down," she said to me. "I mean it. He ain't as well as he wants to think he is. And you," she said with a toss of her head in Leon's direction, "don't you even be talkin' to me."

"Let's go," Leon said through a grin, so I hopped in the backseat and went while the nurse stood at the edge of the curb with the wheelchair and watched us go.

"You look like shit," I said after I got settled.

"You don't look that great yourself," Leon said. "And you just got back from paradise."

"Lester will keep for a while, you know," I said. "We don't have to do this right now."

"We don't hop right on it, he'll hit us first. He knows I'm never gonna be any weaker than I am right now."

"We don't have to be anywhere he can find us."

"We care about too many people, bro'. He can always find someone."

The truth of those words hammered me back in my seat, and I stayed there without talking for a while. Junior nosed us almost due east from the hospital, and after a few minutes he stopped in front of Leon's place on Sixteenth.

"You know what to do?" Leon asked.

"Yeah," Junior said. "I'll be there."

"Keep your eyes open while you're waitin'. He sends more than one car there, you're gonna wanna know about it."

"I've got it covered, boss. You just make sure you don't put yourself back in the hospital."

"Ain't no way I'm goin' back there. I need to be at full strength before I tussle with those people again." Then he slowly climbed out of the car, only to lean back in with his right hand extended. Junior placed what looked like a nine-millimeter Glock in the hand, and Leon straightened up and checked the gun out thoroughly.

"What's goin' on?" I asked after I hit a button in my door that moved my window out of my way.

"You're gonna have to humor me, bro'. We're kind of on a need-to-know basis here."

"I don't need to know anything?"

"You need to be as much in the dark as Lester. It's safer for all of us that way."

"What do I do?"

"Junior'll drop you at your place. Lester will let you know what to do next."

"Fine," I said, but the word wasn't an accurate description of how I felt, and Leon knew it.

"Just tell him I have his money," he said quietly, "and we'll take it from there."

"Do I have a choice?" I asked.

"Sure," he said. "You just don't have a better one." He slapped the top of the car with the hand that wasn't wrapped around a Glock, and Junior started us rolling south toward Knott Street whether I had anything more to say or not.

"Beautiful," I said, but all Junior did in response was drive.

SEVENTY

Lester was sitting at my kitchen table when I walked in my back door, and so were two other guys I didn't recognize. All three of them had hardware in plain sight, but no one was pointing or pulling or otherwise indicating anything bad was about to happen.

"Honey, I'm home," I said, but Lester didn't respond to that, and neither did his companions.

"Fine," I said. "Be like that. How'd you get in?"

"Bedroom window on the other side of the house," Lester said.

"I don't think I left that open."

"It's way open now."

"How'd you know I was back?" I asked.

"I told you before you left that I take care of my business," Lester said. "Speakin' of which, ain't you travelin' a little light?"

"I don't know," I said. "If I had the money in my hand right now, would I still be alive?"

"Good point," Lester said. "So where does that leave us?"

"How 'bout you turn yourself in, then I deposit the money in your prison account?"

Lester was quick for a man his size. He was out of the chair and in my face faster than I could blink, and as soon as he got there he wrapped his huge right hand around my throat and rammed me against my empty refrigerator.

"Do you think you're cute?" he asked, his mouth so close to mine when he said it that we could have kissed had we been so inclined.

The answer to his question was yes, but I didn't tell him that because his grip on my throat prevented speech. It prevented breathing, too, so I did nothing but stand there and slowly turn blue.

"Where's my motherfuckin' money, Wiley?" he asked finally, and I could tell he wanted an answer this time because he turned me loose as he said it.

"I sent it to Leon," I said, although it took me a while to spit it out.

"Why the fuck would you do that?"

"I thought you might grab me by the throat and take it from me before I had a chance to punish you for your transgressions."

"You ain't got no chance of punishing me," he said. "Why don't you know that?"

"Looks like I do know it, Lester. That's why I sent the money to Leon."

"He's gonna rue the fuckin' day you did that, Wiley."

"Rue?" I said.

"You don't know the word?"

"Yeah, I know it."

"Then you didn't think I knew it," he said, and his big fist flew in so close behind the words that it could have erased them all before I even heard them. It didn't do that, though; what it did was redesign my nose. I jerked my head back instinctively, but he still caught me square enough to pop the cork on my blood supply.

"I'm so tired of that shit," he said as he produced a big blue handkerchief and tried to wipe my blood off his hand. "And of hearin' the name Leon every time I turn around."

When he finished with the handkerchief, he handed it to me. "You're bleedin' all over yourself," he said.

"You had to know this would be goin' through Leon at some point," I said through the handkerchief.

"Motherfucker's in the hospital. What the fuck's he gonna do?"

I tried to shrug in response to that, but the way I was hunched over the work I was doing on my nose robbed the move of the flair I intended. "I don't think you'll like the answer to that question," I said.

"Actually, I've been lookin' forward to this for a long time."

"You had your chance. You already fucked it up."

"When was the last time someone sent him to the hospital?" Lester said. "Leon's runnin' out his fuckin' string, Wiley, and I'm the one's gonna yank it on him."

"You *are* doin' better than anyone else ever did," I said. "I'll give you that."

"Let's go," he said with a curt nod toward the door.

"Give me a minute to take a leak first," I said.

"Let's go. I don't want you bouncin' back out here with your prick in one hand and your fuckin' gun in the other."

I stood in my spot next to the refrigerator without moving for a moment or two, my mind reviewing the options in front of me. A moment or two was all that took, however, so it wasn't long before all four of us were trooping out the door.

SEVENTY-ONE

"Lester wants his money," I said into Lester's phone. Lester was doing all the driving, so I was the designated talker. I had the seat next to him, and his companions were both in the seat behind us.

"Tell him to come and get it," Leon said.

"He says to come and get it," I said to Lester as he pushed a late-model Chevy sedan through a yellow light at Fifteenth and Fremont.

"Fuck that," Lester said.

"He said fuck that," I said into the phone.

"Fine," Leon said. "I can find a use for it."

"He says fine—he can find a use for it."

"Fuck that, too," Lester said.

"He says fuck that, too."

"Tell him to call back when he has something else to say," Leon said.

"He says to call back when you have something else to say," I said to Lester.

"Just tell him his little buddy is toast unless my money shows up at the park next to Madison within the next thirty minutes."

"Uh-oh," I said into the phone. "He says I'm toast if you

don't send his money out to the park next to Madison within the next thirty minutes."

As soon as the words were out of my mouth, Lester cracked me with the back of his right hand. My head bounced off the padded seat behind me, and my mouth suddenly filled with blood.

"You think I'm playin' here, motherfucker?" he asked.

"Perish the thought," I said as I spit into the same blue handkerchief he had given me in my kitchen.

"What?" Leon said into my ear.

"Lester hit me," I said into the phone. "The big meanie."

"Give me the fuckin' phone," Lester said, and he snatched it out of my hand before he finished saying it. "Make that twenty-five minutes, motherfucker," he said to Leon right before he cut the connection and started punching another number.

"I want all three of you at the park next to Madison in fifteen minutes," he said into the phone. "And be ready to fuckin' do somethin' when you get there."

"Callin' in the Three Stooges?" I asked when he tossed the phone into the cup holder between us. "You got the number for Abbott and Costello, too?"

"If you think your entertainment value's gonna keep you alive, Wiley, you might as well sit back and relax. I don't find you all that amusin'."

"You can't get ahead in show business like that," I said. "You gotta keep pluggin' away until you catch your big break."

"So what happened to Dannyboy?" he asked, as though ignoring my attempts at humor might make them go away.

"He capsized while kayaking," I said. "Kind of tragic, really."

"Sounds like it," he said. "Just don't expect somethin' similar today. This rig ain't gonna flip over in the parkin' lot out here."

"You never really know, Lester. That's up to the gods."

"There ain't no fuckin' gods."

"That's the same thing Danny said."

"Fuckin' Danny couldn't tie his own shoes," he said as he guided the Chevy through the intersection at Forty-second. "Believe this, at least—I ain't Danny Alexander."

"Lester," I said, "that I *do* believe. You're not pretty enough to be Danny."

"Jeezus Christ!" he said. "I swear to God I'd smack you again if you didn't bleed on me every time I do it."

"You can't have it both ways, Lester. It's incongruous to deny the existence of the gods in one sentence and swear to them in the next."

"Actually, you *are* kind of amusin'."

"I've been telling people that for years."

"Yeah, I'll probably chuckle every time I look back on this experience."

"I don't know, Lester. You wanna look back on this, you better get back on the fuckin' phone."

SEVENTY-TWO

It took Lester less than fifteen minutes to hit Eighty-second and only a minute more to turn south and cruise to the park next to Madison High School, which meant we were crowding midnight by the time we got there. I saw three cars in the parking lot, but the only one I recognized was Lester's old Suburban.

Lester parked two spaces north of the Suburban and shut the Chevy down. I could see signs of life in the other car when I looked through Lester's window, but there was nothing between my window and the Dairy Queen across the street at the north end of the lot. I turned my attention to Lester when he started fumbling under his seat, but as soon as I got a look at the additional handgun he came up with I started looking for something else to watch.

That's when the phone in the cup holder rang. Lester looked at it for two or three rings before he picked it up, and his face almost immediately indicated that he should have waited a lot longer.

"You're fuckin' crazy if you think I'm gonna play ring-around-the-rosy with you all night," he said into the phone. "You think this is a fuckin' joke?"

I had no idea what was flowing into his ear, but he didn't

speak again. After another moment or two, he lowered the phone and looked at me.

"Motherfucker don't care if you bake or broil, Wiley," he said.

"He cares," I said. "What he doesn't care for is negotiating."

"He says Junior has the cash down at the Safeway parking lot. We want it, we have to go down there for it."

"Well, we all know you want it."

"Yeah," he said slowly. "We all know that." Then his voice trailed off while he sat there for a moment or two, and when it came back he pointed it at the guys in the backseat.

"Look," he said. "He's movin' us down to the Safeway parkin' lot. Get in with the guys in the Suburban, and tell 'em to drive down there in front of me. There should be a Mercedes sittin' there with its lights on. Park right next to it, but make sure you're pointed so you can see the entrance. I'll come in a couple of minutes after you."

Lester leaned back in his seat while his companions exited the car and moved to the Suburban, and a moment later the Suburban's headlights came on and it drove out of the lot. It turned south on Eighty-second, and when it disappeared over the crest of the hill in front of the high school, Lester turned his attention to me.

"Junior brings the cash to your side of the car, then puts it where you're sittin' when you get out. Think you can do that?"

"If the gods are willing," I said.

"I don't really know that fuckin' Junior," he said. "Is he gonna try to cowboy this thing?"

"Junior pretty much does what he's told," I said, but what I didn't say was that neither of us had a clue as to what that might have been.

"So all I have to worry about is the motherfucker in the hospital."

"And me," I said.

"And the fuckin' gods."

"Yeah," I said. "Them, too."

"Fuck it," Lester said. He cranked up the Chevy, rolled it out of the lot, and pointed it south. He didn't say a word during the four or five minutes the trip required, and I said exactly what he said. What I did instead of talk was marvel at the amount of traffic on Eighty-second around the witching hour on a Saturday night, but I have no idea what he was doing until he slowed down as we approached the entrance to the Safeway lot.

I immediately began looking for Junior and the Mercedes, and I know Lester was doing the same thing, because neither of us gave the Lincoln Continental waiting to make a left turn into the lot a second glance. Spotting the Mercedes behind its headlights next to Lester's Suburban was easy, but it took me a split second to locate Junior because he wasn't in the car—he was coming at the Suburban from the opposite side with something in his hands that looked a lot like a shotgun.

Lester was halfway through his turn into the lot by the time I saw all this, and that's when the Continental suddenly catapulted forward and slammed into Lester's side of the Chevy. The impact of the collision slammed me against the side of the car, and then the air bag pinned me back against my seat, but after that I lost track of what happened for a moment. I know it involved screaming tires, flying glass, and the rending of metal, and that the Chevy ultimately skidded into the metal pole planted at the edge of the driveway hard enough to collapse the right front corner of the car on top of itself.

The first thing I did when I caught up with all this was

check on Lester. He was pinned into his seat by his door on one side and the air bag in front of him, but he seemed to be having no trouble raising the gun in his right hand. Then my door flew open and Leon jammed his Glock right in front of my face.

"Put it down," he said, his voice surprisingly quiet considering the circumstances. It wasn't too quiet to get through to Lester, though, because he took one look at the Glock and lowered his arm again.

"Take the gun and get out of the car," Leon said, and I did one and then the other.

"Fuck," Lester said. "That was one helluva move."

"Yeah," Leon said as he leaned into the space I had vacated and pressed the Glock to Lester's right temple.

"It was never personal, man," Lester said matter-of-factly, his eyes staring straight into the air bag in front of him. "You know that, right?"

"No, Lester," Leon said. "I don't know that at all." Then he did something to the Glock that made the far side of Lester's fat head explode.

I remember all that like it happened in slow motion, but what followed might have been on fast forward. First the Suburban roared out of the lot, then Junior pulled up to us in the Mercedes. We both sprawled into the backseat, and we were rolling north before we got our heads up high enough to see out of the windows.

"I didn't know you could still move that fast," I said as soon as I was physically capable of speech.

"Adrenaline's a wonder drug," Leon said softly. "There's nothin' else quite like it."

"Do you know how many witnesses there were to what just happened?" I asked.

"No," he said. "But I wouldn't worry about it."

"Why not?" I said as Junior turned west where Eighty-second runs out of road at Killingsworth.

"We both saw it all," Leon said, his voice still soft and low. "What do we need witnesses for?"

SEVENTY-THREE

"This is fuckin' bullshit!" Sam said, and there was enough heat rising off his voice when he said it to boil frozen water.

Sam was right, of course, but he would get no confirmation from me. I leaned back in my chair in Leon's living room, closed my eyes, and tried to imagine myself floating in the arms of a sea serpent somewhere in the Pacific Ocean.

"If that motherfucker was here all night," he said, "I'll eat the fuckin' chair you're sittin' on."

"You try that," I said, "you'll be the next one in intensive care."

"He's not *in* intensive care, though, is he? Just so happens he signed himself out last night."

"You're wrong about him," I said. "You always have been."

"I've got his fuckin' Lincoln with its nose jammed up the victim's ass. Am I wrong about that?"

"Cars get stolen every day, Sam."

"Don't try to get cute, Wiley. I'm not in the fuckin' mood, I promise you."

"You don't want any answers, don't ask any questions."

"I haven't heard an answer yet," he said. I shrugged that off, but I don't know what Sam did, because my eyes were still closed. I was watching the scene at the Safeway unfold again on the backs of my eyelids, and it was no more believable in retrospect than it had been the first time.

As usual, Leon had been lucky. The sound of two cars colliding always draws the attention of everyone within earshot, but I could tell from Sam's frustration that he had yet to find anyone at the scene who actually knew what the fuck had happened.

Other than me, of course, but I wasn't at the scene by the time Sam got there, and I wasn't talking, anyway.

Not that Leon was home free, exactly. Junior had the job of making the gun and the surgical gloves disappear, so that could always go wrong somehow. And Leon still had Sam sitting in his living room, where Sam was chewing on me like he hadn't eaten in a week.

After a while, I succeeded in blocking Sam out of my mind. I focused instead on an old woman I had never met and probably would not like who had lived in the hills overlooking the city with a son who had never grown up—a son I was now certain never *would* grow up.

In my mind's eye, I had only one thing in common with this woman, one terrible and devastating thing, which made my heart go out to her in spite of myself.

"You can go in now," Leon's private nurse and primary alibi said suddenly from the edge of the room, "but please make it short." I was up and moving before the last word was out of her mouth, and I could feel Sam's hot eyes all over me as I crossed the room.

"This shit isn't over," he said. "Tell him that."

"I will, Sam," I said. "You know you can count on me." I kept walking until I escaped through the door to the room Leon was using and left Sam and his eyes behind me.

"Sam says this shit isn't over," I said.

"Imagine my surprise and consternation," Leon said.

"You're crazy, do you know that?"

"Maybe," he said. "Mostly, I think I'm just tired."

"Well, you have plenty of time to rest up. Sam won't let go of this anytime soon."

"How about you?" he asked. "You look a little beat-up."

"Something happened to me over there," I said, "but I don't think you can see it. I might have to go back for a while."

"What's up?" he said.

"I don't know, exactly. I met someone I want to get to know, but I'm not even sure if that's it."

"Could be the place itself, bro'. I think you've been needin' it for a long time."

"Maybe," I said. "It's kind of funny, though. In a lot of ways, it didn't seem that different from being here."

"Except for the Hawaiians, right?"

"How'd you know that?" I asked.

"Please," he said, his eyes closing for a moment while he drew the word out a little. "Junior's got the money you sent over if you want it. For some reason, Lester didn't ever pick it up."

"That might come in handy," I said. *"Mahalo."*

He smiled wanly at that, then looked a little more closely in my direction. "The money won't last forever, though," he said. "And there aren't any legal cardrooms in Hawai'i."

"Yeah," I said. "I know. I guess I'll have to figure that out, won't I?"

"Something else is on your mind," he said, his careful scrutiny continuing to pay dividends.

"Danny's mom," I said, although that was only one of several things on my mind. "I just hope I can find the right lie by the time I get up there."

"You don't have to lie," he said. "His kayak capsized and

he drowned in the ocean. Tears were shed both here and there, end of story."

"You might be right," I said.

"Or crazy," he said. "Take your pick."

SEVENTY-FOUR

THE COLUMBIA RIVER GORGE EAST OF
PORTLAND, OREGON, JULY FIFTEENTH

Everyone was there except Leon, who was still stuck in his sickroom with Sam crawling all over him like a—well, like a homicide detective.

It was Leon who had gotten James there, though, and it was James who had led us up and down the trails near the falls until Mr. and Mrs. Jones couldn't take it anymore.

"I'm really sorry," James said. "It was dark at the time. All I can say is, he's out here somewhere."

"We appreciate you tryin', son," Mr. Jones said. "We really do."

"Do you have any other questions for James?" I asked.

"No," Mr. Jones said. "Ah guess we understand what happened as well as anyone can."

Genevieve began to weep out loud at that point, and Ebony leaned in close and absorbed as much of Gee's grief as she could. They rocked together for several moments, and it wasn't long before the Joneses were doing exactly the same thing. Then Alix, Ronetta, and Julie joined with them, and I was left standing to one side of the group with James on the other.

The group eventually shifted, and everyone ended up

holding hands in a strange, elongated loop that barely fit into the confines of the trail. Then we all bowed our heads as though responding to the same celestial cue, and Mr. Jones began to pray.

"Dear Lord our God," he said, "please raise our boy Ronnie from this wood where he lays and clasp him to your heavenly bosom. Keep him safe from the storms of this world until we all come to meet him in your glorious presence. In the name of Jesus Christ our savior, amen."

"Amen," we all answered together, and then James started slowly back down the trail. Everyone moved off behind him at a pace suited to Mr. and Mrs. Jones—everyone except Julie and me. She stood next to me with her hands jammed into her jeans, her face turned toward the falls.

"Not much water this time of year, is there?" she said.

"No," I said.

"It's still beautiful in here, though," she said.

"Yes, it is," I said, and then both of us dropped talking in favor of soaking up the scene around us in silence.

"How are you?" I asked finally.

"All the bad guys are dead now, right?" she asked.

"Yes," I said.

"Does that make you feel any better than you did before?"

"Not really."

"Me, neither," she said. Then she turned and started down the trail, and I stood there and watched until she disappeared into the dense green canopy with the others.

SEVENTY-FIVE

Alix was the only one still in the parking lot at the head of the trail when I got there. She was leaning against the side of her Tercel with her arms folded loosely across the front of her chest, and she watched me through her unreadable black eyes as I approached.

I watched her right back as I came, still stunned that such a woman had ever waited for me. "God, you're beautiful," I said quietly, as though her beauty had a special volume all its own and needed none from me.

"I'm a grown woman, Wiley," she said. "Spit it out."

"I don't know what to say."

"You used to teach the English language, right?" she said, more than a little edge in her voice. "Fucking think of something."

I continued to stare into her eyes while I thought, but nothing came to mind until a single tear rolled down the right side of her flawless face. I reached over to wipe it away, but she shook my hand off before I got the job done and continued to let her high beams bear in on me.

"Something happened to me over there," I said finally.

"Some*thing* or some*one?*" she asked.

"Both, maybe."

She nodded her head as though agreeing with something,

but her eyes did not have a drop of acquiescence in them. "I knew this day was going to come from the beginning," she said after a moment of silence. "You'd think I'd be ready for it."

"I'm not saying I know what it all means," I said.

"Would that I were so lucky."

"What's that supposed to mean?" I asked, my voice the one with a little edge in it this time.

"I'm just another woman you were willing to die for, Wiley," she said softly. "It sounds like you may have finally found one you're willing to *live* for."

The truth in that statement chilled the heat in me with only the slightest of effort, but I wasn't immediately ready to concede it. "Maybe," I said. "But I think there's more to it than that."

"Such as?" she said.

"I think it goes all the way back to my father, or maybe even farther."

"Your father is dead, Wiley, and so are all the fathers before him."

"Not over there," I said. "I think I may still have access to them over there."

"That's an interesting point," she said, "even if it is off to the side a bit."

"What?"

"This is about fucking, Wiley, plain and simple. You can't fuck me, and you might be able to fuck this new one. Maybe you already have. Ironic, huh?"

"Don't say that, Alix."

"No, I mean it. The hooker who fucked half of Portland loses her man because he can't fuck her. I find that ironic, to say the least."

"That's not the least you could have said."

"I know it," she said, tears streaming unimpeded down

both sides of her face now. "Don't even listen to me, okay? We've all been hoping you'd reach this point someday, so don't pay any attention to me."

"Would that I were so lucky," I said, wrapping both of my arms around her and holding on for all I was worth. "You *compel* attention, baby, especially from me."

"I can't promise I'll be waiting for you if you come back," she said into my chest as she blotted her eyes on my shirt.

"I know," I said into the tight blonde curls on the top of her head. "I can't promise I'm coming back."

"Okay, then," she said, tossing her head and stepping away from me. "That's all settled. All you need now is a ride back to town."

"No problem," I said, even though her Tercel was the only car in the lot. "I'm Hawaiian, you know. I probably have my outrigger parked down by the river."

"You better climb in with me, sailor," she said with a faint fascimile of a smile as she opened the door of her car and slid behind the steering wheel. "The way I heard it, you have trouble keeping those things afloat."

"Literally and metaphorically both, actually," I said, and then I walked around the car and entered it from the opposite side. I leaned toward Alix and she leaned toward me until our lips met in the middle. After a sweet moment at that intersection, we both buckled ourselves in for our first ride in the general direction of wherever we were going next.